MURDERS
ANONYMOUS

By E. X. Ferrars:

MURDERS ANONYMOUS

PRETTY PINK SHROUD

BLOOD FLIES UPWARDS

THE CUP AND THE LIP

ALIVE AND DEAD

HANGED MAN'S HOUSE

THE SMALL WORLD OF
    MURDER

FOOT IN THE GRAVE

BREATH OF SUSPICION

A STRANGER AND AFRAID

SEVEN SLEEPERS

SKELETON STAFF

THE SWAYING PILLARS

ZERO AT THE BONE

THE DECAYED GENTLE-
    WOMAN

THE DOUBLY DEAD

THE WANDERING WIDOWS

SEEING DOUBLE

SLEEPING DOGS

FEAR THE LIGHT

DEPART THIS LIFE

COUNT THE COST

KILL OR CURE

WE HAVEN'T SEEN HER
    LATELY

ENOUGH TO KILL A HORSE

ALIBI FOR A WITCH

THE CLOCK THAT WOULDN'T
    STOP

HUNT THE TORTOISE

THE MARCH MURDERS

CHEAT THE HANGMAN

I, SAID THE FLY

NECK IN A NOOSE

THE SHAPE OF A STAIN

MURDER OF A SUICIDE

REHEARSALS FOR A MURDER

MURDERS ANONYMOUS

E. X. FERRARS

PUBLISHED FOR THE CRIME CLUB BY

DOUBLEDAY & COMPANY, INC.

GARDEN CITY, NEW YORK

1978

All of the characters in this book
are fictitious, and any resemblance
to actual persons, living or dead,
is purely coincidental.

Library of Congress Cataloging in Publication Data

Ferrars, E X
Murders anonymous.

I. Title.
PZ3.B81742Mw 1978 [PR6003.R458] 823'.9'12
ISBN: 0-385-13536-X
Library of Congress Catalog Card Number 77-89881

MURDERS
ANONYMOUS

CHAPTER ONE

It was going to be one of Kate's bad mornings. Matthew knew it as soon as he woke up and saw her sitting on the edge of her bed, gripping it as if it were a life raft, while she stared into the distance as if she had seen smoke on the horizon which might promise her rescue. But the bedroom curtains, in a yellow and white pattern that she and Matthew had once chosen together, were all that she could see.

Dull daylight seeped through the curtains. It fell on her tense face, faintly oily from the cream that she had rubbed into it the evening before, and was reflected in her wide, dark, angry eyes. She had woken up angry, for whatever reason Matthew, as always, was unable to guess. In some way, whenever this happened, he took for granted that he was to blame, though she never told him just how or why he was. Distantly, silently, she would carry the dark secret of how he had offended her throughout the day, only, apparently, all of a sudden to forget it herself and become relaxed, casual, even loving. Less and less loving as time passed, yet it could sometimes happen still.

It was all very mysterious to Matthew, and very painful. He was a man who blamed himself easily for the unhappiness of others, a quality in himself that he had failed to recognise as a kind of egoism. In his diffident way, he saw himself as affecting other people far more potently than he actually did. Usually he tried to deal with his incomprehensible guilt by saying nothing, showing nothing and hoping for the best, the best being that somehow, without explanations, without apologies on either side, the emotional temperature would change. This morning, as he went on watching Kate under half-closed eyelids, he hoped that she would not notice that he was awake until she had thrust her feet into her bedroom slippers, stood up, coiled up her long, dark hair and made for the bathroom.

She was a tall woman, slender, thirty-two years old, more beautiful than she had been when they had married five years ago. Matthew also was tall and was bony and slightly stooping, with a round, mild, gently intelligent face, wide-set grey eyes and smooth brown hair that was beginning to recede above the temples. He was fifteen years older than Kate.

When he heard water running in the bathroom he let his eyes close and slipped into a half-doze, eager to escape briefly from the sense of hazard that a glimpse of Kate in one of her black moods always gave him. It was only when he had heard her go downstairs to get breakfast that he got up himself, trailed yawning into the bathroom, showered, shaved and dressed. From the amount of noise that she was making in the kitchen he knew what to expect when he followed her down, either an electric silence, or else—and it was the alternative that he disliked the more—a stream of questions about how he expected to spend the day. They would be spoken in a half-strangled voice of desperate self-control, with a total indifference to his answers, and would give him the horrible sense of a storm brewing. Yet for some strange reason the storm never burst, at least until he was out of the house. Perhaps Kate sat and cried then for hours, all by herself. Perhaps she took to smashing the china, hurling it violently about the kitchen, then later sweeping it up and quietly replacing it without having told him what she had done. Perhaps . . . Perhaps . . . How could he guess what she did when he was not there to see her?

He went into the kitchen, a roomy, shiny place, full of all the gadgets that any heart could desire. He sat down at the table and, when she slammed the coffee pot down in front of him, murmured, "Thanks."

She sat down facing him and poured out coffee for herself. She was wearing a loose dressing gown of soft, deep purple wool. The sleeves fell back, showing her white arms when she put her elbows on the table. Leaning her head on her hands, as if she had a headache, she stared broodingly into her cup without starting to drink the coffee. Her dark hair fell forward between her fingers. They were so tense that it looked as if she might be finding it difficult not to tear the hair out by the roots.

Matthew put butter and marmalade on his toast and began to eat it.

After a moment she suddenly raised her head, looked at him sharply and said, "Well?"

"Yes?" he said. "Well?"

"What are you doing today?"

He always answered her carefully if it was one of her days for questions.

"I've a lecture at ten," he said, "then I've a meeting of the Works Committee at eleven, then I've got to try to find time to see one of the research students about twelve o'clock, then I'm having lunch in the Volunteer with Colin—"

"Colin?" she exclaimed. "Is he in London?"

"Apparently."

"Then why isn't he coming here for the night?"

"I think he's going home. Naturally I asked him to stay when he telephoned yesterday, but he said he was only coming up for the day."

"Then why aren't you bringing him to lunch here?"

Matthew drank some coffee. "I think actually he wants to talk to me on my own and I think I know what about. You'd find it boring. And I didn't want to bother you to lay on a meal."

"But I like Colin."

She made it sound as if Matthew had deliberately deprived her of a pleasure, though she did not usually show any signs of desiring the company of his brother-in-law, Colin Naylor, the husband of Matthew's elder sister, Cornelia. Colin was a senior lecturer in molecular biology at the new university of Godchester, an amiable, easy-going man whom Kate had never found it important to cultivate.

"He suggested lunch in the Volunteer himself," Matthew said. "I don't suppose he's got the time to come all the way out to Golders Green."

"What's he doing in London?"

"He's giving a paper to the Royal Society this afternoon."

"What does he want to talk to you about?"

"I'm afraid it's Barraclough's chair. You know Barraclough's going to Berkeley in the autumn. I think Colin wants to ask me if there'd be any point in his applying for it."

Barraclough, of whom Matthew spoke, was professor of molecular biology at Welford, one of London University's many colleges, where Matthew was professor of genetics. Everyone knew that Barraclough was leaving and that his chair would be vacant, though it had not been advertised yet.

"And has Colin any chance of it?" Kate asked.

"I don't think so. I think they've got someone else lined up." He stood up, glad that in another few minutes he would be out of the house. This was a feeling which had grown on him rapidly in recent weeks and which, when he noticed it, scared him.

"Are you going to tell him so?" she asked.

"I expect so. The appointment's still confidential, but I can at least advise him not to waste any time over it."

"I suppose he thinks you might still be able to help him."

"I doubt it. He knows how these things are done as well as I do."

"Could you have helped him if you'd tried in time?"

"I did try, as a matter of fact, but I didn't get anywhere with it."

"I wonder how hard you tried." Her lips twitched faintly in a sceptical little smile. She slid the tip of her tongue along them. "The truth is, you aren't very good at helping people, are you, Matthew? You find it a bit too much of a bother. D'you know, I once thought I could lean on you. I thought you cared. Isn't that strange?"

"Why don't you try it sometime and see what happens?"

"When you speak in *that* tone of voice?"

Her dark eyes suddenly blazed at him. For once, he thought, the continuous anger that simmered in her under the surface and that was destroying her was going to boil over. She was really going to lose her temper. She really wanted a quarrel.

And then, perhaps then, when they had had out into the open all the hatred that they could endure, they might achieve some sort of reconciliation. Was that impossible? Was it too much to hope that somehow, sometime, after some such quarrel, if there was no other way, they might even rediscover what they had once loved in one another?

But after only an instant Kate dropped her eyes and a look almost of fear passed over her face, as if she had just looked over a brink into an abyss and found what she saw there terrifying. Standing up swiftly, she slipped out of the room.

As she passed Matthew, she said, "You'll be late for your lecture."

He heard her run upstairs. And he recognised that if he did not hurry he would indeed be late for his lecture.

He put on his overcoat, which was hanging on a peg in the narrow hall of their semi-detached house, collected the briefcase that contained his lecture notes and started out down the road towards the Underground station. He walked with long, loose-limbed strides. The March morning was cold, with a damp wind blowing in his face, and until his fast walking had warmed him the chill penetrated to his bones. It must have rained in the night, for he had to skirt wide puddles on the pavements and the bare branches of trees in the gardens of all the other semi-detached houses along the road shone with a dark, greasy-looking gleam. There were snowdrops and aconite in some of the gardens and a few almond trees were in bloom, their blossoms looking too fragile to withstand the tossing that the wind was giving them, yet mysteriously surviving it. A sky of thick, hurrying cloud hung low above the roof-tops.

The road was a long one. When Matthew and Kate had first come to live here he had generally gone by car to Welford College, which was on Haverstock Hill, but parking problems had made him change his habits. Today the walking, battling with the wind, had the fortunate effect of almost driving out of his memory that moment when he and Kate had seemed to come near to facing the disaster of their marriage. The truth was that there had been many such moments recently and nothing desperate had ever come of them. So that was probably how things would go on. Seeing the milkman near the end of the road, delivering milk bottles on to doorsteps, Matthew as usual said, "Good morning."

"Hallo, Mr. Tierney," the man answered. "Shocking morning."

"Not very nice, no," Matthew agreed.

"Forecast last night said sunny intervals and warmer. Can't ever trust them, can you? Don't know why we bother to put it on or why we bother to listen."

"Perhaps the sunny intervals are still to come," Matthew said.

"No, it was yesterday we had those," the man reminded him. "Haven't you noticed the way they tell you yesterday's weather's coming tomorrow? Always doing it. An insult to our intelligence, that's what it is."

He went on grumbling to himself as Matthew continued along the road that led to the station.

His own words echoed oddly in his head. "Sunny intervals are still to come. . . ."

But the milkman was dead right, you were a fool if you believed it, as Matthew had believed it over and over again, not specifically about the weather, but rather about the clouds that hung over his whole life. Perhaps he tended to do this simply for the sake of his own immediate comfort. Naturally it was easier to face a day if you felt that there was a chance that it would brighten presently. As occasionally it did. All days were not equally bleak. Arriving at the station and feeling in a pocket for his season ticket, he passed through the barrier and got on to a train for Hampstead.

He lectured badly that morning. He was not consciously thinking of Kate, yet he could not concentrate. He knew it from the amount of fidgety scraping of feet on the floor that he could hear and the gradual increase in the amount of coughing. He was boring his audience. He was boring himself too, feeling that there were few jobs as unrewarding as lecturing to a big roomful of first-year students who failed to understand why, since what they wanted to study was physiology or ecology or systematics, they should have a course in genetics thrust upon them.

However, the faculty meeting after the lecture was more boring still. An incredible amount of time was spent in arguing whether or not a concrete path should be laid between the Botany and Zoology buildings. Some people seemed to hold quite emotional views on the subject and to be ready to talk about it almost indefinitely. Others were so indifferent that they sat back in their chairs and appeared to let their minds go wandering off into private dreams.

Then, when the meeting was at last over, Matthew had to talk to a Ph.D. student who wanted his help in obtaining a grant to go to a conference in Luxembourg. The boy happened to be singularly intelligent and also, as Matthew had noticed, was uncommonly addicted to hard work, so he promised to do what he could to help, though he found the boy's wispy beard and stained clothing very unattractive. But the dreadful unattractiveness of so many of the young of the moment was something against which he had had to learn to steel himself. Luckily, he knew, a good many of them would grow out of it sooner or later. Putting on his overcoat, Matthew promised his secretary that he would return in the afternoon to deal with the correspondence that he ought to have dealt with the day before, and set out to meet Colin.

The Volunteer, where they had agreed to meet, was a pub near Tottenham Court Road. Colin was already there when Matthew arrived, sitting at a table in a corner with a mug of beer in front of him. He was a short man with a lithe, springy body, wide shoulders, a bullet head and a ruddy, healthy face with a square jaw, a short nose, a mouth that smiled readily and excellent teeth. His thick, black hair stood up from his forehead in short curls. He looked far less than the forty-eight that he was.

His friendship with Matthew went back through most of their lives. They had been at the same grammar school, then at the Imperial College, London University, and though Colin was two years the older and that gap between their ages had seemed a far greater gulf then than it did now, it had somehow never seemed important. Matthew had always been rather old for his age and Colin, as he was to this day, very youthful. He had been a brilliant student. He was given a First in his degree and a notable future had been foretold for him. Only he had always been a little too fond of sailing, of going fishing in Scotland, of climbing mountains, for the future to have materialized. His marriage to someone as serious as Cornelia, when they had known each other for half their lives and never shown a great deal of interest in one another, had taken Matthew quite by surprise, though it had delighted him. They lived in a flat in the rather dreary small town of Godchester, but also had a cottage by the sea, where they spent weekends and vacations and which made it possible for Colin to maintain the glowing tan that looked so surprising on a chill March day in London.

He and Matthew bought sandwiches, Matthew ordered a beer and they carried them over to the table where Colin had been sitting. They exchanged the questions that they usually did on first meeting. How was Kate? How was Cornelia? How were things in general? According to both of them, everything in their lives was fine. Yet each, viewing the other with the eye of old intimacy, perceived that the answers meant very little. There was tension in both of them, more in Colin even than in Matthew, which was unusual. The ordeal ahead of him, reading a paper to the Royal Society, of which he was not a fellow and never would be, as Matthew had been for the last two years, seemed to be on his mind. Colin had never been a skilful performer. He had an acute mind, which he could use with a good deal of success on anything that happened to interest him, but it worked unpredictably. Questions confused him. He seemed to feel that he would never have anything to say that could be of much account to anyone else. Today, besides, he had not only his lecture on his mind, but another matter to which he got around after his second beer.

"Of course you know what I want to talk to you about," he said.

"Barraclough's chair, isn't it?" Matthew answered.

A shade of embarrassment passed over Colin's face. "I don't want to bother you, but Cornelia thought I ought to talk to you about it. It's just a question of whether you think there'd be any point in my applying. Or starting to think about applying. I'm not even sure if I really want to, but Cornelia feels I ought to look into it."

"Actually, I think it's already fixed up," Matthew said, "unless the chap backs out at the last minute. I believe he's got reservations about coming to live in London."

"Do you really think he might back out?"

"I've heard it said that he might."

"Then perhaps I ought to apply after all."

Matthew struggled with himself for a moment. He shrank from crushing a hope. But in the end there would not be much kindness to Colin in telling a lie, for the truth was that even if the man now expected to step into Barraclough's shoes should back out on account of the expensiveness of living in London and the discomfort of having to spend an hour or two a day travelling to work, Colin had not a chance of being considered in his place. Professionally he had gone as far as he ever would.

"Honestly, I don't think there's very much hope,"

Matthew said. "But you wouldn't much like working in London yourself, would you?"

"I loathe the place," Colin replied. "But of course we'd keep the cottage, and if Cornelia wants a change . . ." He shrugged his shoulders.

"Well, I wish I could be more encouraging."

"In fact, you're telling me not to apply, aren't you?" One of Colin's engaging smiles lit up his face. "That's that, then. I can tell Cornelia in good faith that I did my best, can't I? You'll back me up when I tell her I haven't a hope?"

Matthew started to laugh. "You don't want the job, then?"

"My God, no!"

"Then why . . . ?"

"Oh, from time to time Cornelia gets an attack of pushing me to be more ambitious and I get the feeling I've let her down by being too satisfied with a merely comfortable life. We've a very comfortable life, you know. I can walk to the lab. in ten minutes and they leave me in peace there to do more or less what I want. We've plenty of friends in Godchester and we can drive to the cottage in an hour. Which reminds me, are you and Kate coming down to the cottage any time this vac.? We'd love to have you."

"Thanks, I'd like to, but I'm not sure. . . ." Matthew paused. He looked away into the crowd of heads around the bar. After a moment he went on, "Colin, tell me something. You know when Kate stayed with you at the cottage in December after that attack of flu she had."

"Of course."

"Well . . ." But Matthew was already regretting having started on this subject. He had not come to meet Colin meaning to confide in him. Usually, of the two of them, Colin was the more likely to pour out his troubles, though these were generally of a minor kind and had a way of curing themselves without Colin's having exerted himself much to deal with them. But a great pressure had been building up in Matthew's mind since the morning, which forced words out of him almost against his will. "Well, did anything special happen to her while she was with you?" he asked.

"Happen?" Colin said, looking blank.

"Yes, I mean . . . It's difficult to say what I mean, but I've been very worried about her lately. It's almost as if around then her nature changed. That'll sound absurd to you, but when she came home after those three weeks she'd spent with you, she seemed almost a different person. She seemed—I'm bad at putting this kind of thing clearly—but everything about her that sometimes used to be a bit difficult seemed to have got wildly exaggerated. It's very strange. She's become so hostile suddenly that sometimes I feel I can't stand it much longer, mainly because I can't understand it. So I wondered if anything could have happened to upset her while she was with you. Did you notice anything strange about her? Do you think Cornelia could tell me anything? They've always been quite good friends."

Colin rubbed a finger along the edge of his square jaw.

"She'd just inherited her aunt's money, hadn't she?" he said. "She'd become a rich woman."

"Why should that upset her?"

"I don't know. But money does have an odd effect on some people sometimes. For instance, are there things she could do now with all that money which she feels you're preventing?"

"I don't see how she could. We've hardly discussed it. It's hers to do what she likes with."

"What has she done?"

"Nothing much so far. Bought a few clothes. A nice ring. A dish-washer. Talked of having fitted carpets for the whole house. She doesn't seem to want to move to a larger house, or buy a new car, or go in for mink. I've suggested we might go abroad in the spring vac. to Madeira or Mexico or somewhere, but she didn't seem enthusiastic."

Colin nodded with an absent look on his face, as if he were trying to focus on some image a long way off, as far away as that cottage by the sea where Kate's strangeness had developed.

"Of course, she did have her portrait painted while she was with us," he said after a time.

"Ah, that portrait!" Matthew muttered. "I was forgetting that. She paid for it herself, of course, I'm not sure how much."

"You don't like it?"

"I hate the thing. But she seems very pleased with it. To me it's a horrible caricature of her, but she somehow manages to find it flattering. So I don't see how that could have affected her."

"Except that portraits don't paint themselves, you know."

Colin was still looking into the distance, as if now he were anxious not to meet Matthew's eyes.

Matthew felt his heart give a sudden sharp thump in his chest as if something very frightening had just happened. Yet after a moment, when the sensation had passed, he heard himself saying in what he believed was a normal voice, "The artist, Grant Staveley, you're telling me he's at the back of it."

Colin brought his gaze back to Matthew's face. "No, I'm not telling you anything," he said. "But you asked if anything special happened while Kate was with us, and those were the only things I could think of, her aunt's money and the portrait. Incidentally, Staveley's got a show on at the Crowther Gallery next week. He's busy getting things organised there now. We came up on the train together this morning. Cornelia and I have been staying at the cottage for the last few days for peace and quiet while I finished writing this damned paper."

"She's never told me much about him," Matthew said. "He's a friend of yours, is he?"

"Just a neighbour. He lives in that white house—d'you remember it?—up on the cliffs. He moved in last year."

"Ah yes."

But for the moment Matthew could not visualise the house, though he knew that he must have passed it countless times on the walks that he liked to take in the evening along the cliff path during the visits that he and Kate often paid to the Naylors' cottage.

A white blur of a building, seen usually in the twilight, that was all that came to his mind now. He was not observant when he went walking. What he enjoyed about it was the way that its rhythm set his mind working, helping him to find answers to problems that had troubled him all day, problems perhaps connected with research, or with the administration of his department, or with difficulties with people. At such times, if he noticed anything he passed, it was more likely to be a flower in his path or a rabbit scuttling into its burrow than a house or even a human face.

Yet the thought of whiteness remained hauntingly in his mind.

After a moment, he said, "A queer thing, you know. Kate's recently developed a mania for white flowers. She's always bought a lot of flowers for the house and nowadays they're always white. White roses, white lilac, things like that. I just happened to realise it the other day. Isn't it a rather strange thing?"

"Must come a bit expensive at this time of year," Colin remarked.

"Yes, well, she can afford it and she enjoys it," Matthew

said. "She's clever with them. She arranges them beautifully. But nowadays they're always white."

"A lot of people don't care much for white flowers, d'you know that?" Colin said. "Apparently they connect them with death and funerals. I heard somewhere that the sale of them goes up enormously in a flu epidemic."

"Of course it isn't important."

"It sounds a pretty harmless foible to me."

"But in that portrait, d'you remember, she's holding some white flowers in her lap? The thing's too abstract for one to be able to recognise what they are, but they're a bunch of something white. I never thought of connecting the two things before. Staveley, I mean, and the flowers."

Colin stirred uneasily. "I wish I'd never said anything about him."

"Don't worry. I know it probably doesn't mean anything."

Yet after Matthew and Colin had separated and Matthew was in the Underground train on the way back to Hampstead, he found himself unable to stop thinking about the portrait, about the white flowers and Grant Staveley. He was a shadowy figure about whom, now that Matthew came to think it over, Kate had said surprisingly little. She usually liked to talk about the people she met, describing them with an entertaining and often malicious vividness. In fact, she very seldom talked about anything but people. She hardly ever allowed herself to become bogged down in discussions of abstract subjects which she did not understand. But she had said next to nothing about Grant Staveley, with whom she must have spent a fair amount of time while the portrait got itself painted.

Matthew did not know if the artist was old or young, tall or short, good company or what she considered dreary. But he had painted Kate with white flowers in her hands and now the house at Golders Green was always full of white flowers. So the man seemed to have had some influence upon her and there was nothing ridiculous in brooding on them, even if it had been a blunder to talk about them to anybody else.

Matthew spent the afternoon as he had promised his secretary that he would, dealing with the correspondence that had been accumulating on his desk for a number of days. He dealt with a good deal of it by pitching it into the waste paper basket. He had a theory that if you simply threw most of your letters away, someone or other would sooner or later ring you up about anything that had been important. Then a minute or two on the telephone would get you further than a bothersome exchange of letters. But he had never induced his secretary, Miss Graves, to see eye to eye with him on this. She was a little wisp of a woman of nearly fifty who looked as if she lived in a perpetual state of fright, though the truth about her was that she was driven through life by a relentless sense of efficiency, a respect for order which gave her a backbone of steel, and she had long ago established a ruthless ascendancy over Matthew. He never argued with her, only at times, with great cunning, escaping the demands that she made upon him.

This afternoon, to her great satisfaction, he settled down to plough through letters and forms as she placed them in front of him, but even she could not keep his attention from wandering. It was difficult to keep it on the workaday problems of the department when he was asking himself if his wife had a lover. Or if not actually a lover, then a man in her life important enough to ruin her relationship with Matthew. A man much more important to her than Matthew had ever been, for he was sure that he had never caused her such disturbance of heart and mind as she seemed to be suffering now. And now that this thought had occurred to him, it seemed amazing that he had never considered it before. Extraordinary, complacent, childish. For it explained everything.

And perhaps because it explained so much, it brought him a curious feeling of calm. Gazing out of the window at some plane trees, hearing his own voice dictating, he reflected that he was far less distressed than he would have expected. Here was something that could be grasped. It could be discussed. Something could be done about it. He need not go on struggling unavailingly with his sense of guilt at having somehow incomprehensibly failed her. None of it was really his fault. It was just one of those things that happened to people about which you could be reasonable.

Naturally he would agree to any arrangement she wanted. Had she really thought that he would not? Was that why she had treated him to all those scenes of smothered hatred? How much easier it would have been for them both if only she had told him the truth. Now they could settle everything. There need not be any difficulties about money of the kind that can bring disgusting sordidness into the break-up of a marriage. She had her inheritance, he had his salary. It would all be straightforward.

Of course, if he loved her, as he had always supposed that he did until recently, he might find it harder to be so reasonable. . . .

"Professor—" Miss Graves's small, firm voice broke in on his musing.

He wondered how long he had been silent.

"I'm sorry," he said. "Where were we?"

"You're writing to the dean. '. . . writing to submit proposals . . .'"

"Oh yes. '. . . for departmental expenditure for the next year. . . .'"

He went on dictating.

It was about six o'clock when he reached home after walking more briskly than usual up the long road from the station. He was sustained by the feeling that there were practical steps that could be taken to put himself and Kate out of their misery. The evening was colder than the morning, but the wind had died and the sky had cleared, with frosty stars glittering in the darkness, and the chill did not strike nearly as deeply into him as when he had left the house. Yet as he approached it his steps became slower. After all, what was he going to say to Kate? Since leaving the college he had rehearsed half a dozen different ways of opening a discussion with her without having made up his mind which would be best. For suppose she refused to discuss anything with him. Suppose she did not want to leave him. Suppose she denied everything, said that there was no other man, that Grant Staveley meant nothing to her. Suppose even that this was true. . . .

He put his key into the lock and opened the door.

There were no lights on in the house, which might have been the reason why he instantly had the feeling that it was empty. But he was sceptical about such feelings, thinking how often they turned out to be misleading. One remembered only the occasions when they had been right. The times when they had been wrong were easily forgotten.

Going into the sitting room, he turned on the light there.

He had not been wrong. Kate had left the house, had gone, would never return. The living Kate with her bewildering secret. It was only her body that she had left behind. It lay on the floor, her eyes and her tongue protruding, her face dreadfully discoloured, and with a cord drawn tight round her throat.

CHAPTER TWO

You called the police. That was the first thing to do. You did it at once.

But Matthew found himself sitting in a chair, possessed by a fearful lassitude, which made the telephone on the table by the fireplace seem as remote as if it were poised on a distant planet. His arms and legs felt heavy and useless. He did not feel sure that they would move when he told them to. Sitting still, he let time pass and almost forgot about the necessity of making that telephone call.

He knew that he had bent over Kate, had touched her, had called out to her, begging her not to be dead. But the lifeless thing on the floor had been cold and stiff and unresponsive. It had been only for a moment that it had seemed to have any true connection with Kate. After that it had become something frighteningly preposterous, a mocking unreality. Perhaps, he thought, he had been unconscious for an instant, for he could not remember collapsing into the chair. But now that he was there it seemed profoundly pointless to try to get out of it.

The room with its window facing the street and its french doors at the other end that opened on to a small garden was just as usual, except for Kate, rigid on the hearthrug in front of the low brick fireplace. It was a pleasant room with several easy chairs covered in dull russet tweed, a soft green carpet, a good old walnut bureau in one corner and two walls covered with bookshelves. In a vase on a small round table under the window was a bunch of narcissi.

White, of course.

Matthew could not remember for sure, but he did not think that they had been there the day before, so it looked as if Kate had been out to the shops that morning before her murderer came. He took this in without being much interested in the fact. To his stunned mind nothing seemed of any interest or importance except for the overwhelming fact that Kate was dead. The room in which he had once taken a quiet sort of pride and known contentment had become a grotesque place, desecrated to the point where it no longer mattered.

The most grotesque thing there was the portrait over the fireplace. Matthew had never understood why Kate had been so pleased with it. Was it just that she had been flattered at having been painted at all? In her place Matthew would have considered the picture an insult. With a malicious kind of insight, only just avoiding caricature, the artist had given her a vapid, self-satisfied face with a small, meaningless smile on it as she looked down at the white cloud of flowers on her lap. She seemed to be sitting on a stool that did not appear in the picture and was wearing the dark red sweater and black slacks that clothed her dead body now. The paint was thick and rough on the canvas, which somehow increased a blurred look of emptiness about her features that seemed to have been the main thing about them that the artist had tried to convey. But that emptiness was not the truth about Kate, or only a part of the truth. Matthew found himself hating the portrait more than he ever had before and suddenly feeling a wild lust to snatch up some weapon and slash at it.

To stop himself looking at the painted face, he at last got up out of his chair. He had no idea how long he had been sitting there. Perhaps it had been only for a minute or two, or perhaps for half an hour. Going to the telephone, he dialled 999, asked for the police, told the voice that answered him that he wanted to report a murder, gave his name and address, spoke calmly, thanked the disembodied voice that told him that the police would be with him in a few minutes, and put the telephone down.

Then he rushed out of the room. He could not have stayed there a moment longer. He had been terrified by the sound of his own calmness while he had been speaking on the telephone. It had not been sane. Surely it would have been normal to rave and shout. And he had not yet shed a single tear or felt any real grief. What had happened to him? Was it simply that his emotions were numbed, as his feet felt strangely numbed and spongy under him, or had shock dried up his humanity at the source? How much true humanity, if it came to that, had he?

He went to the dining room, thinking that the normal thing to do at a time like this would be to give himself a drink. A stiff whisky. Only he did not really want one. He was rather afraid of the effect that it might have on him. Presently, perhaps, but not just now. Leaving the dining room, he wandered into the kitchen and saw Kate's shopping-basket standing unemptied on the table.

So it had been true, as the flowers had told him, that she had had time that morning to go to the shops before she met her death. What had he been doing at the time, he wondered, when her murderer had called here? Lecturing, listening to a dull argument about a concrete path, talking to the boy who wanted to go to Luxembourg, having lunch with Colin? Whenever it had been, he had felt nothing. Wasn't that strange? How could she have experienced the intense terror of her death and not the slightest pang of uneasiness troubled Matthew?

He was still in the kitchen when the police car stopped at the gate. Two young men in uniform came to the door. He thanked them vaguely for having come so quickly, hardly hearing what they said, and as they muttered something back to him which he did not take in, led them into the sitting room.

He heard them both catch their breaths at what they saw and one of them turned very pale. A look of fascination appeared on the face of the other. But it was the pale one who spoke.

"She's your wife, is she, sir?"

"Yes," Matthew answered.

"When did you find her—like this?"

"I think it was about six o'clock."

Matthew and the young constable glanced simultaneously at their watches. It startled Matthew to find that the time was half past six. He had sat in that chair, doing nothing, for longer than he had realised.

"How long have you been out?" the constable asked.

"All day. It was about a quarter past nine when I left the house."

"Where did you go?"

"To Welford College. I work there."

It struck Matthew suddenly that the two men were looking at him with a certain wariness, which he thought for a moment was due to concern for him. He was probably looking very distraught, ready to collapse on their hands. Then he remembered having heard that when a man or a woman is murdered, the first person to be suspected is always the spouse.

The thought filled him with a weary kind of dismay. He was certain to be questioned very thoroughly sooner or later, though not, he would have thought, by anyone as junior as these two. But whoever undertook the questioning, he was not certain how much of it he could stand without breaking down, and he found the thought of breaking down among a lot of suspicious strangers horrible. You didn't give away your feelings to strangers.

"Did you notice anything . . . unusual . . . before you came in here and found your wife, sir?" the pale young constable went on.

"Unusual?" Matthew asked uncertainly.

"A door or a window open. Anything disarranged. Anything at all."

"No, nothing."

"I suppose you haven't had time yet to find out if anything's missing. Jewellery or money or anything valuable."

"No, I hadn't even thought of looking," Matthew said. "When I found her I think I passed out for a little while, then I telephoned the police and then just waited for you. Why? Do you think that's what happened? I mean a burglar. That she came in and disturbed him. There's nothing particularly valuable in the house."

"There doesn't have to be. There are people who kill old women in the dark, on their way home from bingo, just for the few quid they've got in their handbags."

"My wife had a little jewellery," Matthew said. "Shall I see if it's still there?"

"I'd wait till Superintendent Mellish gets here," the constable answered. "He'll be taking charge. Meanwhile, if you don't mind my saying so, sir, I'd go and sit down." Something kindly came into his voice. "There's nothing you can do in here. Is there any whisky in the house?"

"Yes, but I don't want anything."

"I'd have some all the same. You look as if you could do with it."

"Yes, well, perhaps . . ." Matthew turned to the door.

The young man who so far had said nothing went with him as he made his way back to the dining room on his spongy feet. He watched with absorption as Matthew poured out a large whisky and subsided into a chair. Taking a quick gulp, Matthew immediately felt that he was going to be sick, but the spasm passed.

"This your first murder?" he asked as the young man lingered in the doorway.

A deep blush covered his simple, eager face.

"'Smatter of fact, it is," he said.

"Mine too." Matthew drank some more.

"Yes, of course, sir," the young man said.

"You'll get used to it, I suppose. All in the day's work. This Superintendent Mellish now, what kind of man is he?"

"Oh, very capable, sir."

"An experienced man, then. Accustomed to the smell of evil. Breathing it in daily, so used to it, perhaps, it hardly repels him any more. You can get used to any smell, you know, from violets to a sewer, so that you hardly notice it any more."

"Yes, sir."

Matthew frowned. He must stop this. He was talking like an idiot. The thing to do was to sit there drinking his whisky slowly and wait to do whatever talking he must to Superintendent Mellish.

He arrived about a quarter of an hour later, a very tall man, taller even than Matthew and very much broader, a fact that was exaggerated by a too tight suit, which clung to his bulging muscles in deep creases. He had a big, square face with features that were oddly neat and small, little restless eyes under shaggy, sandy eyebrows and sandy hair which was curly and thick above his forehead, but showed a bald patch further back. His age was probably in the early fifties. It was unfortunate that Matthew immediately took a dislike to him.

He did not want to dislike him. He wanted to give all possible help to him in his inquiries. He struggled against his own reaction to the man, doing his best to put down his instant feeling of aversion to his own state of shock, which might be giving him an excessive sensitivity. But presently, when he and the Superintendent were facing one another across the dining room table and the Superintendent had begun to put to him quiet, courteous, direct and sensible questions, Matthew could not convince himself that this big man would ever listen to any answers, that there was any point in trying to tell him anything but the barest outline of the truth. He felt that it was impossible to talk seriously to anyone who seemed so complacently secure in himself, with such obviously blunted perceptions and lack of subtlety.

Not that subtlety seemed to be needed now. One of the men who had arrived with the Superintendent, and there seemed to be a great many of them to judge by the voices and the amount of tramping up and down in the small house that Matthew could hear, had discovered almost at once that there were clear signs that someone had got into it by the kitchen window. There were some scratches in the fairly new paint on the windowsill and a few muddy footmarks on the linoleum leading towards the door. Matthew himself had discovered that all Kate's jewellery was gone, except for a diamond ring, which was the only valuable thing that she possessed and which she had bought for herself recently, after inheriting the hundred thousand pounds that had come to her from her aunt. That ring she happened to be wearing now. She had worn it almost constantly since she had bought it and at this moment it was sparkling on her right hand.

"You can see what it looks like," Mellish said in a bland, impersonal voice when Matthew had given him a description of the jewellery that was missing. "He got in, this character we want, by the kitchen window when your wife had gone out shopping. He took all the jewellery he could find and he may have been just about to leave when she came in and found him. He lost his head then and instead of making a bolt for it, which would have been easy enough for him, she being just a woman and alone, he killed her and was too panic-stricken when he'd done it to think of taking that ring off her finger. Now can you tell me, Professor, was your wife in the habit of leaving that kitchen window open when she went to the shops? There are no signs of the latch having been forced."

"I think she may have been," Matthew answered, "if she didn't mean to be long."

"So he climbs in, shuts the window behind him, goes straight to the place where ninety-nine women out of a hundred keep their jewellery, that's to say, a drawer in her dressing-table, comes down and was going to let himself out by the door when she came in and disturbed him. A very tragic thing. It so nearly needn't have happened. If she'd met a neighbour who'd kept her chatting for a few minutes he'd have got clean away and she'd still be alive. And even if we hadn't found the jewellery, which we may still do even now, there'd have been the insurance. It was insured, I suppose."

"Yes, but only for a couple of hundred. The diamond ring was insured for two thousand."

"I'm interested in that ring," Mellish said, "its being so much better than anything else she had. What was it, an anniversary present, something special in that line, or an investment, or had you come into money?"

"My wife had come into money," Matthew replied.

"Ah, had she now? A lot?"

"It seemed a lot to us. About a hundred thousand. An aunt of hers died last year and left all she had to her."

"And who inherits that now?"

"I do, I suppose." It was the first time that that had occurred to Matthew. "We both made wills soon after we got married, leaving all we had to each other. Not that either of us had anything but odds and ends at the time."

"And your wife didn't alter her will when she came into money?"

"Not that I know of. Why should she?"

"Oh, she might have felt inclined to leave legacies to friends, or something of that kind. I was just wondering, you see, if there's anyone besides yourself who benefits by her death."

"Then you don't really believe in this man who came in by the kitchen window," Matthew said. He began to feel a throbbing in his head. His hands, lying on the table before him, went rigid.

"Oh, I do, I do," Mellish assured him, "but one's got to think of everything. There's only one thing against it. The common type of prowler, the sort we've been talking about, apart from the fact that he isn't usually a killer, would have had to notice that open window from the street, if it *was* open, before he came in to try his luck. But you can't see that window from the street, it being at the side of the house. So what brought him in?"

"What do you mean?" Matthew asked. "If it *was* open? I thought you were sure that he came in that way."

"Not sure, not a hundred per cent sure," the big man said. "It's too early to be sure of anything. Some other character could have come to the house, perhaps even been let in by your wife herself, then made those marks on the windowsill and the floor to delude us. That's been done before now. And if it was like that, you can see he might even have been someone your wife knew. So it's natural to ask if there's anyone who could have had a motive. Who gains?"

So perhaps the man was more subtle than he had seemed.

"Is gain the only motive?" Matthew asked.

"Can you suggest another?"

Matthew suddenly found Mellish's small eyes boring into his as if they were trying to see inside his skull. He resented it intensely. His skull and its contents were very private property, not to be inspected even by someone with a search warrant. He closed his eyes briefly to shut out that intrusive stare, then said with a sigh in his voice, "Isn't it about time you asked me for my alibi?"

"I was coming to that."

"Purely as a matter of routine, isn't that what you should say?"

"Of course, sir." Mellish appeared not to have noticed any irony in Matthew's voice. "If you'd prefer to tell me how you spent the day, we can get that matter out of the way."

"When was my wife killed?" Matthew asked.

"We'll be able to tell you a little more exactly after the post mortem," Mellish said. "The most we can say at the moment is that it was probably in the latish forenoon, say between eleven and one. We think she'd been dead for at least six or seven hours when you called us."

"In that case I was either at a faculty meeting, or talking to a student, or perhaps I'd already gone out to lunch."

"Let's have how you spent the whole day, shall we?" Mellish said. "Begin with when you saw your wife last."

"I saw her at breakfast," Matthew said. "I left the house about nine-fifteen."

"Anyone see you leave?"

"I don't imagine so. I did exchange a few words with the milkman, but I don't suppose he noticed the time."

"Your wife didn't walk along to the shops with you?"

"No, she was still in her dressing gown when I left. She must have got dressed later."

"Where did you go?"

"To Belsize Park station. I took the train to Hampstead, walked down Haverstock Hill to Welford College, gave a lecture from ten to eleven, then attended a meeting of the Works Committee—I talked to several people there, they'll remember me—then about twelve o'clock I interviewed a student called Jones who wanted my help with a grant he's after to go to a conference, and after that I took the Underground to Tottenham Court Road, met my brother-in-law, Colin Naylor, at a pub, the Volunteer, and had lunch with him there. I should think it was about two o'clock when we separated. I went back to Welford and spent the afternoon dictating letters to my secretary, Miss Graves, packed that in about half past five and came straight home and—and found . . ."

"Thank you," Mellish said quickly. "That's very nice, very complete. This brother-in-law of yours, now, where does he live?"

"In Godchester. He's a senior lecturer at the university."

"He was on a visit to London?"

"Yes, he was giving a paper to the Royal Society. He was only up for the day. I'm not sure if he went back to Godchester in the evening—his address there is 12 Canonby Crescent—or to a cottage he owns down by the sea in a village called Fernley. His address there is 1 Cliff Walk, Fernley. If you want him to corroborate what I've said you'll find him at one or the other place."

"Then that seems very clear. You understand, we'll have to check it all."

"As a matter of routine."

"Routine, routine," the big man said. "Nine tenths of my job. Yours too, I shouldn't be surprised. Nine tenths of most people's jobs. And where would they be without it? Running round in circles, chasing their tails. Now perhaps you can help me with what you think your wife would have done after you left the house. She'd have got dressed, I suppose, and tidied up the house a bit, made beds and so on and then gone shopping."

"She might have, or she might have done the shopping before the tidying up," Matthew said. "She liked to get to the shops before they filled up."

"Can you tell from the things she'd bought where she'd been?"

"More or less." Matthew had taken a look at the contents of the basket that Kate had left on the kitchen table. "She went to Gittin's, the grocer, and to the greengrocer, Chorley, and she also went to one of the flower shops, I'm not sure which, and bought those white narcissi you probably noticed in the sitting room."

"She bought those today, did she?"

"Yes, they weren't there yesterday."

"Well then, she came home and she put the flowers in water straight away, though she didn't bother to unpack her basket of groceries, perhaps she was just going to start on that when she heard him. He'd have been hiding upstairs. They didn't come face to face as soon as she got into the house, because, if they had, she'd never have had time to put the flowers in water. But she'd done that and I suppose taken off her coat too. She'd have worn a coat when she went out shopping, wouldn't she? She wouldn't have gone just as she is now."

"No, she generally wore a sheepskin jacket for shopping," Matthew said. "It's hanging on a peg in the hall now."

"Yes, I saw it. So she had time to do those two things—"

"No!" Matthew said, suddenly alert. "You've gone wrong. It can't have been like that. Not if she died between eleven and one. I told you, she nearly always did her shopping early. She'd probably have got dressed quickly and left the house about nine-thirty, quite soon after me. She'd have got to the shops in about ten minutes, done that shopping in, say, twenty minutes, come back—another ten—and that brings the time to only about ten-fifteen. And if all she had time to do was take off her coat and put the flowers in water before she was attacked, it doesn't fit. It makes the time of her murder far too early. Besides, there's the question of when she stacked the dish-washer and made the beds."

Mellish stroked the bald patch on his head. "I was wondering if that would strike you. I agree, it doesn't fit too well. But you've got to remember we may be wrong about the time of her death. It's a thing you can't ever be really accurate about. That's why, as a matter of fact, I'm very interested in those shops she went to. It may be that someone in one of them will turn out to be the last person we can find who saw her alive, and that may come in useful. Suppose, for instance, she varied things for once and did her tidying up first, then went shopping later than usual. One never knows what may turn up. Well, thank you, Professor, I think that's all for the moment. You've been very helpful."

Matthew in his turn also muttered thanks and went upstairs to his small study, just then the quietest place in the house, and as soon as he sat down was seized by a fit of helpless shaking, which went on for several minutes and left him feeling as if every scrap of strength he had had been drained out of him.

He could not imagine how he had managed to talk to the Superintendent so calmly. The memory of it gave the whole interview a kind of falsity, as if between them they had carefully avoided saying any of the important things that might have been said. Not that Matthew knew what they were, but their ominous shadows seemed to stir vaguely somewhere just below the surface of his consciousness. He found that he had not the slightest faith in that burglar.

But if not the burglar, who?

And did Mellish believe in him?

It was midnight before all the men who had been occupying the house with their flash bulbs, their fingerprint outfits, their all too casual voices and their heavy feet, at last left it empty. Kate's body had been taken away earlier and all that was left of her now was a chalk outline on the hearthrug in the sitting room.

Mellish had advised Matthew not to remain in the house for the night. Hadn't he friends, he had asked, who would give him a bed? Yes, of course, several, Matthew had replied, but he thought that he would prefer to stay where he was. At home. Only the house was not home any longer. He realised that as soon as the policemen had left him there alone. Home had been something shared by himself and Kate, and even if in recent times it had become a place which he had liked to avoid as much as possible, it had still stood for something important. But now, in its emptiness, it meant nothing.

He had eaten nothing since he had arrived home that evening and as soon as he was left to himself he discovered that he was painfully hungry. But apparently it was mostly a nervous hunger, for when he had made himself a thick sandwich with some cold beef that he found in the refrigerator, he could hardly force it down. Some coffee went down more easily. He drank several cups of it, knowing that so much was likely to keep him awake, but since he did not expect to sleep in any case, what did it matter? He stayed in the kitchen, wondering if he would ever be able to make himself use the sitting room again. Even with Kate's body removed, that mocking portrait of her would go on leering down at him with its stupid, empty eyes. He would have to get rid of the damned thing soon, sell it or perhaps just cut it into pieces and stuff it into the dustbin.

He thought what an odd thing it had been in a way that he should have been able to give Superintendent Mellish such a very full account of how he had spent the whole day. Whatever happened now, no one was going to be able to suspect him of having murdered Kate. Not all of his days were so fully occupied. For instance, he might have had lunch by himself in one of the pubs near the college. He often did. He might even have spent most of the day at home, working on a paper with which he had been struggling in a rather desultory way for the last few weeks. But, of course, if he had done that the murder would not have happened, since Kate would not have been alone in the house. Unless an end would have been put to him too. Did that seem probable?

A curious sense of guilt because Kate had been the victim while he had escaped slid like a train of fog across his mind as he sat in the kitchen with the half-eaten sandwich on the plate before him and his fingers folded around the cup of hot coffee. But the guilt went beyond that simple fact. That morning at breakfast Kate had appealed to him, or gone halfway to appealing to him for help. Then somehow something that he had said or done had made her feel rebuffed and she had quickly turned the appeal into a sneer and he had escaped from the house as soon as he could. And wasn't that going to haunt him for the rest of his life? Whatever depths she had been floundering in alone without confiding in him, she might still be alive if he had made her talk to him. The fullness of his day proved that there was no possibility that he had committed the murder, but hadn't he been an accessory before the fact? Leaving her in the way he had, hadn't he left the door wide open for her killer to enter?

Only metaphorically open, of course. It had probably been Kate herself who had opened the door to him and perhaps even welcomed him in. For that burglar was a myth. What burglar, looking for jewellery, would have left the diamond on her finger? However terror-stricken he had been at what he had done, he would have grabbed it.

So the murderer had been someone whom Kate had recognised and let into the house. Someone she perhaps had expected, perhaps loved, perhaps feared, or at the very least had trusted. And his reason for killing her? Could Kate somehow have been a menace to someone? Matthew finished his coffee and at last went up to bed.

He slept as soundly as if he had been drugged. Perhaps that was what shock did to you. He did not waken until about nine o'clock the next morning, coming up slowly out of dreamless sleep to a sense of total disbelief in everything that had happened the evening before. It was only when he had gone downstairs in his dressing gown and seen the chalk outline on the hearthrug that stood for Kate, and the grey smears of fingerprint powder everywhere, and had smelt the stale cigarette smoke left behind by the detectives, that the comforting disbelief faded. He made himself more coffee, toasted some bread which he burnt but which he nevertheless spread with butter and marmalade and gulped down in a few bites. The chief question on his mind at the moment was what to do about the day ahead of him. Should he go in to the department? Should he telephone Ron Carter, an assistant in it, to tell him that his wife had been murdered and that he did not feel up to working today? Or perhaps that he was just feeling ill? He shrank from the thought of his grim news spreading like wildfire through the college and would have preferred to stay quietly at home without touching the telephone. But soon the police would be going to the college to check his alibi, the press might follow them, and rumours worse than the truth would probably start to circulate. Reluctantly, he reached for the telephone.

Of course, once the story was out, there was no hope that he would be left in peace. Soon the telephone began ringing incessantly, and the doorbell too. Sometimes it was the police and sometimes reporters and sometimes colleagues, offering him sympathy and making generous offers of help if only he would tell them of anything, anything at all, that they could do for him. He never could think of anything, unless it was to prevent other people calling up, so he mumbled thanks, cut the conversation as short as he could and resigned himself to wait for the next call.

It was midday when he had a call from Cornelia. She did not bother to say who she was, because she knew that he would recognise her very clear and rather high-pitched voice.

"Matthew, in God's name, why didn't you telephone at once?" she cried. "Yesterday. Last night. As soon as you found her. We could have driven up straight away to be with you. But we've only just heard it from a policeman who came here to check on that lunch you had with Colin. Listen, we're coming now. You needn't put us up. We'll go to a hotel somewhere and take you with us. You oughtn't to be alone. Oh, Matthew, we're both so terribly sorry."

"No, Cornelia, wait a moment," Matthew said in a state of confusion. "Please don't come. I'm very grateful to you, but for the moment honestly I want to be alone. I don't think I could stand anything else. So you won't come, will you?"

"But just Colin and me," Cornelia protested.

"I know, but all the same . . . I'm immensely grateful to you, but until I've got a few things sorted out in my own mind, I think I'd better stay by myself."

"I don't understand," she said. "Are you sure? Because

the first thing Colin said when he'd finished with that police-man was, 'We'd better get up there.' And we're ready to come at once."

"I know, and it's very good of you, but there's nothing that you can do, there really isn't."

"Couldn't we ward off the press and that sort of thing?"

"They aren't bothering me too much."

"You wouldn't like just to have your hand held?"

"I think I may want that later, when I've begun to take in what's hit me. For the moment, no."

"Well, if you're really sure . . ." She hesitated. "Will you come to us as soon as you feel like it? We're at the cottage, and though Colin will be coming and going a bit till the vac. starts, I'll be staying here. You could come here and be perfectly quiet for as long as you like. Do think of it, Matthew."

"Yes, I will, I'd like that. But there's the inquest to come first, and I've got to see our solicitor, and I want to find out when I can put the house up for sale. I want to get some ideas about my future."

"It's awfully unwise to make plans when you're in a state of shock," Cornelia said. "If I were you, I shouldn't make any at all, except to come to us as soon as you feel like it."

"Yes, I'll do that, I promise. I'll let you know when in a few days. And Cornelia, thanks for ringing. You and Colin are always a help."

"Yes, well, good-bye. Take care of yourself, my dear." She rang off.

Matthew put his telephone down, hoping that it would not ring again for at least a few minutes.

However, it went on ringing at intervals for the rest of the day. Also, in the afternoon, he had another visit from Mellish, who seemed now to want to know more than he had the evening before about the Tierneys' marriage. Had it been happy? Was it possible that Kate had ever had a lover? Had there been any area of her life about which Matthew had sometimes felt that he did not know as much as he might?

Matthew looked blank, shook his head and said that he thought their marriage had been ordinary enough. Perhaps if Mellish had been a different kind of man Matthew might have tried to answer him differently, but to offer intimacies to that shallow-eyed hunk of muscle was not to be thought of.

The telephone calls gradually became fewer. From about six o'clock on they ceased. Matthew found some steak in the refrigerator and grilled it with a tomato, ate it in the kitchen, then took a strong whisky and water up to his study, sat at his desk, found a pencil and a sheet of paper and prepared to make notes about everyone of whom he could remember Kate ever speaking. He imagined that there would be a great many things to write down. But nothing came except a few meaningless doodles. Meaningless? They all looked remarkably like flowers. Not recognisable flowers, any more than those that Kate was holding in her lap in her portrait were recognisable, but certainly belonging to the plant kingdom. So perhaps not meaningless. They stood in his mind, rightly or wrongly, for Grant Staveley. Who had been in London the day before. Colin had told Matthew that they had travelled up from Fernley together.

Suddenly the telephone rang again. Matthew put out a weary hand and picked it up.

"Yes?" he said.

A voice that he did not know said, "How much did you pay that brother-in-law of yours for that alibi yesterday? I'd like to know that."

Then immediately the dialling tone started.

CHAPTER THREE

When the first sense of disgust, the sense of having been brushed by something unclean, had passed, Matthew asked himself who could possibly know about the alibi. The police did, of course, and so did Colin and Cornelia. But no one knew better than Colin and Cornelia that they had not been paid for it. Who else knew of it, then? Not the press. Not any of his colleagues. So far as he could remember, he had not spoken about his lunch with Colin to anyone, either before or after it.

No, that was wrong. He had spoken of it to Kate.

He gripped the pencil with which he had been doodling his flowers and, with a sudden, fierce gesture, snapped it in half.

He wondered if it was conceivable that the police would descend to playing a trick on him like that anonymous call. If Mellish had made up his mind that Matthew was guilty and that therefore there must be something wrong with his alibi, his lunch with Colin was the obvious point at which to attack it. But did the police do things like that? Would even as devious and ruthless a man as Matthew could imagine Mellish might be ever go quite so low? Wouldn't he simply have had inquiries made at the Volunteer, learnt that the two men described had certainly had lunch there the day before, and after that, albeit perhaps reluctantly, have accepted the fact that Matthew could not be guilty and started looking for the murderer elsewhere?

His thoughts returned to Kate. If she had spoken of that lunch to anyone, it had been to her murderer. If he had been someone whom she had let into the house, if she had sat and talked with him for a while and told him that her husband and his brother-in-law were out to lunch together, the murderer would know what Matthew had been doing at that time of the day, and was about the only person who would.

But why he should have made that telephone call was another matter. Matthew could find nothing rational in it. Perhaps it was nothing but unreasoning vindictiveness. Perhaps in some way it was intended to frighten him. Or perhaps it was only the beginning of something. There might be more to come which would make the motive clearer.

Meanwhile a sensible person would telephone the police. Wasn't that what you were always advised to do about anonymous telephone calls? But Matthew had had more than enough of the police for the time being. If there were any more calls, he thought, he might tell them then, but at the moment the best thing to do seemed to be to go to bed.

Hoping that the caller would not turn out to be of the kind that takes pleasure in waking you up at two in the morning, yet with a kind of nervous impatience for another call, almost a desire for a chance to enter into a conversation with the man who he was sure was Kate's murderer, Matthew turned off the light in his study and went to his bedroom.

But sleep did not come as it had the night before. It came only in snatches, made horrible by dreams. He almost preferred the periods of tossing in his rumpled bed to the gruesome fantasies of his nightmares. It was when he had just started out of one of them abruptly that he realised that there was something that he had forgotten when he had been enumerating the people who knew of his lunch with

Colin. He had forgotten that Colin had travelled up to London from Fernley with Grant Staveley and that it would have been natural enough for Colin to have dropped a remark to the artist about having arranged to have lunch with Matthew.

He lay still for a while after that, suddenly cured of his restlessness. But presently he began to think that he was letting himself become obsessed by the image of Staveley and not really for any reason except that he did not like his portrait of Kate. Hardly a good enough reason for suspecting a man of murder. All the same, staring blindly into the darkness round him, Matthew tried so hard to imagine what Staveley was like, seeing him in one shape and then in another, that the effort at last gave him a period of relatively quiet sleep. When next he woke, daylight was filtering into the room through the yellow and white curtains. Getting up, he put on his dressing gown and went downstairs to make coffee and once more burn the toast.

As soon as he had had breakfast, he telephoned Cornelia.

The moment that she heard his voice she interrupted him. "Oh, Matthew, I was just going to ring you. We've decided to come to London whatever you say. Now, please don't argue. It can't be good for you, being alone. You needn't be afraid we'll bother you in any way. We'll just be there if you need us."

As she spoke Matthew realised why he had felt so positively the day before that he did not want her and Colin to come to him. Colin he might have tolerated, but all his life Cornelia had always known what was best for him, never suspecting how unendurable he sometimes found it.

"No, listen to me a moment," he said. "I want to ask you something. Have you or Colin spoken to anyone about that lunch he and I had together at the Volunteer?"

"Yes, the police, naturally," she answered.

"I mean, apart from the police."

"I don't know. Let me think. I may have done. Yes, I did. I told Tim Welsh about it. Why?"

"Never mind why at the moment. Who's Tim Welsh?"

"A neighbour. Just a boy. A very nice boy. He was here, working on the tallboy in our bedroom, when the police came. He's restoring it for us and we're tremendously pleased with it."

"A boy? A schoolboy, d'you mean? What are his parents like?"

"No, he's about twenty. His mother's dead and he lives with his father and they run the antique shop in the village. He's wonderfully clever with his hands. Charges quite a lot, though. Still, one doesn't mind that if the work's good enough."

"When did you tell him about the lunch?"

"Sometime after the police went. He was working up-stairs in the bedroom all the time they were here and I didn't know how much he'd heard, so I thought I'd better tell him the truth about it before he started spreading some distorted story around. I made it absolutely clear to him that you couldn't be involved in the murder in any way, so don't worry."

"So by now the whole village may know about it." Matthew was surprisingly disappointed that the number of people who might have made the telephone call to him the night before had just been immensely increased and that it was no longer important to find out if Colin had spoken to Grant Staveley in the train. He could have heard about the lunch from a dozen people. "Was it really necessary to tell the boy anything?"

"It was much the best thing to do." There was a touch of asperity in Cornelia's answer. "With the story in the news-papers this morning—I don't know if you've seen it—it was far better to have got in first with our own version than to seem to be trying to hush things up. After all, if you come down here to stay soon, as Colin and I hope you will, you don't want people giving you sidelong glances, wondering if there's any loophole in your alibi. Matthew, please tell me, just what is it you're worrying about?"

"It's just that I had a rather odd telephone call last night," he told her. "Someone knew about my alibi and was casting doubts on it. And except for you and Colin and the police, I couldn't think of anyone who'd even know about it."

She was silent for a moment, then she asked, "An anonymous call, do you mean?"

"Yes. The caller suggested I'd paid Colin to say we had lunch together."

"How horrible!"

"It wasn't pleasant."

"Well, it wouldn't have been Tim. He'd never do anything like that. He's a very straightforward, normal sort of boy. About Ambrose—that's his father—I'm not quite so sure. But no, I can't really imagine it. Was it a man's voice?"

"I think so, but it was a short call and I was so startled that I'm not absolutely sure."

"You've told the police, of course."

"I haven't, as a matter of fact."

"Oughtn't you to do that?"

"I suppose I ought, but I think I'll wait to see if he rings again. Now that I know it might have been any of a number of people, it doesn't seem so important somehow."

"Just pointless malice. Aren't people loathsome? But I dare say it's best not to take too much notice, since he can't actually do you any harm." She paused again. "Well, I'll see you later."

"No," he said quickly. "Wait. I may be moving out today. I'm thinking of going to a hotel. I find I can't stand this house. But I'm not sure where I'm going, so I can't tell you where to find me, and—"

"It's all right," Cornelia cut in with resignation in her voice. "You needn't elaborate. I understand. You really do want to be alone. It's just how you were when you were a child. If ever you got into trouble you went and hid yourself. But you needn't pretend about your hotel. We won't bother you any more. Good-bye, my dear."

She rang off.

Matthew put down his telephone and went upstairs to get dressed.

Cornelia had guessed correctly that he had no intention of going to a hotel. The thought of possibly being recognised and pointed out as the man whose wife had been murdered was even more repellent than that of remaining in the empty house, though its emptiness now was affecting him as an almost physical thing, pressing painfully on his nerves. He never went into the sitting room. But he had more privacy here than he was likely to find anywhere else.

The anonymous caller left him in peace until after the inquest. The verdict had been one of murder by person or persons unknown. It had, of course, been certain that that was what it would be and the affair had been briefer and easier to sit through than Matthew had expected. The ordeal of the funeral remained to be faced. He had made arrangements for a cremation with a firm that described itself as funeral directors, the ancient title of undertakers apparently striking it as crude. The representative of the firm to whom he spoke treated him with heavy, mournful tact, promising that everything should be done in the best of taste. About the price, now? And about flowers? A wreath of lilies and carnations, perhaps?

Matthew was listlessly agreeing when he realised all of a sudden that such a wreath could be white and, with a violence that took the other man aback, said that he wanted red roses.

He had not been back to the genetics department at Welford since the day of Kate's death, but sooner or later, he knew, it would have to be faced. He decided to give himself until after the funeral before returning and pretending to do some work. There would only be a week then until the end of the term, when he would go down to Fernley. Since there had not been another anonymous telephone call he assumed that there were not going to be any more and that the last one had not meant much. Either that nice and normal boy, Tim Welsh, or someone to whom he had spoken had been responsible for it and the motive had been nothing more than a morbid, impersonal desire to hurt.

But at ten o'clock in the evening of the day of the inquest the telephone rang and Matthew heard the unknown voice again.

"You'll have to pay more and more for that alibi, you know," it said. "There's no end to these things once you begin."

Because he was on the alert this time, Matthew took in more about the voice than he had the first time. He thought that it was a man's voice, though there was a falsetto note in it that made it just possible that it was a woman's. In any case, he felt sure, it was disguised.

He spoke quietly. "I paid nothing for that alibi and you know it, so what's your game?"

He hoped that there would be an answer, but after a short pause the telephone at the other end was put down and the dialling tone buzzed in his ear.

He put his own telephone down. Staying where he was, staring at the wall before him, he wondered if it was possible that the caller really believed what he was saying and thought that he had a chance of extorting blackmail. In that case, poor fellow, he had a disappointment coming. It startled Matthew to realise that in a macabre sort of way he was beginning to find the situation entertaining.

Reaching for the telephone again, he dialled the number of the Naylors' cottage.

It was Colin who answered. Matthew began by telling him the time of the funeral and saying that if he and Cornelia wanted to come to it, he would be grateful. Colin replied that of course they would come.

Matthew went on, "Colin, Cornelia told you, didn't she, about that anonymous telephone call I had the other night? Well, I've just had another. The same as before, more or less. What do you make of it?"

There was a pause while Colin considered.

"Nothing very much, I'm afraid," he said after a moment. "Perhaps this sort of thing happens more often than one knows to people who are in the limelight for some reason or other. Someone wants a sensation, tries to frighten you, feels powerful."

"But he hasn't in fact any power. I've nothing to be frightened about."

"No." There was another pause. "My own feeling is that you shouldn't worry about it too much. It's probably just some crank."

"But a crank who's got hold of certain facts."

"Those facts are pretty much common property hereabouts, due to Cornelia's having shot her mouth off rather unnecessarily."

"You think it's someone from your neighbourhood, then?"

"It could be."

"Have you any feeling yourself about who it might be?"

"Oh, we've a number of odd characters in the village. I suppose it might be any of them. But I can't say I've ever suspected any of them of getting their kicks in this kind of way."

"I was wondering," Matthew said, "did you happen to say anything about our going to have lunch together to that artist chap when you travelled up to London with him in the train?"

"Grant Staveley?" Colin exclaimed. "That's a fantastic idea!"

"Is it?"

"Absolutely. Actually I don't remember if I mentioned our lunch to him or not. I may have. But he isn't at all the type to go in for anonymous telephone calls. You can put that idea out of your mind right away."

"It's always said that there's no such thing as a criminal type," Matthew said. "That you can't tell even a murderer by his looks and general behaviour. So do you think you could really recognise the type that would make these calls?"

"I don't know, but I can tell you one thing. If Grant suspected you and me of having concocted the story of that lunch, he'd say so to our faces. Say it pretty abusively too. Get in a rage about it and shout at us. On the other hand, perhaps he wouldn't care about it one way or the other. The one thing he wouldn't do is something maliciously calculated, like making these calls."

"Do you like him?"

"I wouldn't say that exactly."

"What's wrong with him?"

"Oh, nothing, nothing. I don't seem to have anything in common with him, that's all. That doesn't mean I've anything against him. Cornelia rather likes him, I think."

It was always difficult to induce Colin to speak unkindly of other people. Cornelia might be more informative.

Matthew was just about to ring off when Colin added, "What I'm trying to say is, a man like Grant with an outlet in his painting and a nice wife and an attractive step-daughter whom he seems to be very fond of—why should he feel any need to do furtive things? He's not exactly a repressed character. That's what they usually are, isn't it, the kind of people who do that sort of thing and write poison pen letters and so on? Incidentally, he's becoming quite successful. He's got this show on in London now and I believe quite a lot's been sold. I'd keep that portrait he did of Kate, if I were you. It may turn out an investment."

They said good-bye to one another and rang off.

As they did so, it struck Matthew with sudden astonishment that it had never occurred to him that Grant Staveley might be married and have a family. He had been a name in a void. But now he was beginning to have certain human characteristics.

Colin and Cornelia came to the funeral. So did far more people than Matthew had expected. He had omitted to put any notice of Kate's death in *The Times* and had imagined that the ceremony would be completely private. But Cornelia had done some telephoning to Kate's friends and more of these than Matthew knew existed came to the crematorium. He felt shamed by the number of faces that were unfamiliar to him. He had often felt that Kate took depressingly little interest in his work and the people connected with it, but now he had a chance to realise how little he had known of her life.

It seemed to him, though he could not be sure of it, that there was distinct hostility in the way that a number of these people looked at him. It distracted him so much that he paid far less attention to the ceremony than he might have done and Kate had disappeared behind the curtain into the flames almost before he was aware of it.

Afterwards Colin and Cornelia returned with him to the house.

"Well, that's over," Cornelia said. "It may sound callous, but you'll begin to feel better now. Life goes on. You'll have to face that."

It was easy to recognise that she was Matthew's sister. She was not a tall woman, but she had his slender, almost bony build, his serious grey eyes and smooth brown hair. Matthew had always felt that her appearance and her character were complete contradictions of one another. In appearance there was something almost ethereal about her, a look of fragility, of diffidence and uncertainty that had roused the protective instincts in a number of men before she had married Colin. But in character she was one of the most positive and confident people Matthew had ever known, one of the most simply convinced about the rightness of her own opinions. In childhood he had sometimes hated her for it. For several years she had been bigger than he was and had taken advantage of this to knock him about as well as to tell him what she would allow him to think. When he had begun to grow and had shot past her by many inches, as well as developing a far more active mind than she had, she had abandoned her attempt at physical dominance and settled for the merely emotional. Even that, however, she had largely given up since she had married, transferring it to Colin, who was either unaware of it or acquiesced in it without resentment. Matthew had become much fonder of Cornelia since her marriage.

She had cried at the funeral and had been very quiet in the car on the way back to the house. It was in a disorderly state by now, for the Tierneys had never had any domestic help, and without Kate to care for it, dust had already accumulated, newspapers lay scattered about on chairs and on the floor and there were oddments of left-over food here and there on plates which should either have been put in the refrigerator or thrown away. Cornelia automatically ran a finger along a dusty window-ledge, looked at the grey smear on her finger, but did not refer to it.

"I'll make some coffee, shall I?" she said. She was in a neat, rather shabby brown tweed suit which Matthew vaguely remembered having seen at least five years before. She had never had the least interest in her appearance. "We didn't think you'd have bothered with lunch, so we brought some sandwiches. They're in the car. Colin can get them."

Colin obediently went out to the car and returned with a large packet of chicken sandwiches.

Unpacking them, Cornelia continued, "What I think we ought to decide now, Matthew, is when you're coming down to Fernley, because, seeing you today, I'm sure you ought not to stay on here alone. You aren't looking at all well, d'you know that?"

"You wouldn't expect me to be particularly frisky, would you?" Matthew said.

"Of course not. But I don't imagine for a moment you're feeding yourself properly. How are you sleeping?"

"Not very much."

"Are you taking anything for it?"

"No," he said, "I don't want to get started on pills."

"But it might be wise if you took something for a little while. Why don't you talk to your doctor?"

"It's all right, I'll snap out of it soon. You're probably right that I'll feel better now that the inquest and the funeral are over. Now what I've got to face is going back to the department. I've made up my mind to go tomorrow. Then Saturday week, if that's all right with you, I'll come down to Fernley. How about that?"

"Any time you like," Colin said. "But why go back to the department at all? The term's almost over."

"Simply that I'm scared of it, so the sooner I get it over with the better."

"But there's nothing to be scared of," Cornelia said. "People will only be sympathetic."

"That's what I'm afraid of."

But that was not the whole of the truth. Besides sympathy, which he feared because it might break down his self-control, he was afraid of what might lurk behind it, the same sort of hostility, watchfulness and curiosity that he had sensed at the funeral.

That evening the third telephone call came. The voice said, "You want to know what my game is. You soon will."

This time Matthew did not try to answer, but rang off even before the unknown caller.

When the next morning came and he set off for Welford he was in a mood of gloomy aggressiveness, ready to meet hostility with hostility, if it should be necessary. But in fact it was all quite easy. Very few people said anything to him which suggested that they were even aware that he had just been through an appalling experience, and if this silence was artificial, it was obviously well meant and on the whole comforting. The few remarks that were made to him about Kate's death were brief and kindly. Next day he found that everything felt almost normal and by the third day he began to wonder why he had dreaded returning.

He had seen the family solicitor by then, who had advised him not to try to sell the house for a while, since a house where a murder had just been committed was not likely to command a good price. Better to wait a little, he was told, until memories had begun to fade. Meanwhile there was no reason why Matthew should not look for other accommodation for himself, if he felt that he could not go on living in the house. A small flat perhaps would suit him. He could afford it, even without selling the house. He was a relatively rich man now, he should remember.

Matthew thought that the flat was a good idea and on one or two afternoons during the week that followed went to see some house agents to see what they had on their books and even looked at a few flats, but nothing that he saw appealed to him. One of his problems was that he had not really begun to think out yet how he wanted to live, now that he was alone. He only knew that he must make some change soon. When he left the house on the Saturday morning to go to Fernley and pulled the door shut behind him, he wished with a surge of longing that took him by surprise that he need never see it again.

He did not feel like driving and went by train. Fernley was a sprawling village built around a small harbour and had once depended on fishing for its existence. But now summer visitors brought it more trade than fish. Its few boarding-houses along the sea-front called themselves hotels and the one old pub on the quay had been so smartened up that the fishermen who had once used it would hardly have dared to enter it. However, the suburban development that has attached itself to most towns and villages along the coast had all gone inland, instead of stretching itself along the shore, because of the cliffs that humped themselves up on either side of the village. It had been built in a cleft, well sheltered and somehow maintaining, even in the modern world, a feeling of isolation.

A few houses were dotted up the sides of the cliff. The Naylors' was one of them, only a little way above the village, led up to by a steep lane. Their garden reached almost to the edge of the cliff. There was only a path, a dilapidated wire fence and a few yards of rough downland grass between their wall and the drop down to the spray-smothered rocks below. Sea-birds came wheeling in around the cottage, to pounce on the scraps of bread that Cornelia had a way of throwing out for them. Beyond the cottage were two or three other houses, but beyond them the cliffs became too steep for buildings to cling to them. There was a bench up there, Matthew remembered, where he had often sat, watching the sinking sun turn the sea to opal and then the increasing dusk take away its gleam and change it to a soft, hazy nothingness.

Cornelia met him at the station in her Volkswagen. She was wearing slacks, a loose Aran sweater and a sheepskin jacket. She put an arm through Matthew's.

"I've been half afraid you wouldn't come," she said. "You've been so strange lately. I know it's natural, but we're going to try to get you out of it. A lot of people know you're coming and you mustn't be afraid of meeting them."

"I thought I was to have peace and quiet," Matthew said.

"Oh, you'll have plenty of those. But you mustn't get into a habit of hiding. There's proportion in all things. If you hide too much, people may begin to think it's suspicious."

"I don't think I mind how suspicious they are."

"You would really, you know. I suppose you had to tell the police where you were going."

"Yes, I gave them your address."

"Well, I don't suppose they'll bother us." They had got into the car. "Matthew, how much will you mind it if they never discover who killed Kate?"

He had asked himself that question a good many times during the last few days.

"I'm beginning to mind the idea of it less than I did at first," he said. "Sometimes I think it hardly matters. But I expect the police will get him in the end."

She started the car. "Do you know the police trace only a tiny percentage of the people who've committed known murders?" she said. "A man we know in the forensic department at Godchester told us so. He couldn't tell us, of course, how many murders happen without ever being suspected."

"All the same, I've a feeling they'll catch Kate's murderer," Matthew said. "Sooner or later. And it just can't be helped that, until they do, I suppose I'll go on feeling there's a cloud hanging over me."

She gave him a quick glance. "Colin says you asked him a lot of questions about Grant Staveley. Would you like to meet him?"

"Not much," he answered, "though I suppose I should."

"So you do suspect him."

"I may know more about that when I've met him."

"I wonder if you will."

"What does that mean?"

"Just that I've known him for some time now and I don't feel I know anything much about him. Anyway, a feeling isn't going to be enough. You'll have to find some proof."

"I might not bother about that."

"You mean you might not try to get him convicted?" As he did not answer, she waited for a little, then went on, "You haven't any crazy idea that you might take the law into your own hands, have you?"

He laughed. "Oh, God, Cornelia, have I ever been a person for taking action about anything if it could be avoided?"

She gave him an uneasy frown. "I don't know. There's something odd about you at present and I know that's only to be expected, but still . . ."

She did not try to finish what she had started to say, but, turning the car off the main road into the steep lane that led up to the houses on the cliff, drove in at the gate of the cottage.

It was a low building, washed a pale pink and thatched.

The front door opened straight into the living room. One door, opening out of it, led into the kitchen. Another opened on to a steep staircase that led up to the bedrooms above. A bathroom had been built on at some time beyond the kitchen on the ground floor. It was all fairly primitive, but the Naylors had made the living room gay with hand-woven rugs on the stone floor, blue curtains at the two small windows set deep in the thick walls, wicker chairs with bright cushions, and a fine old dresser, covered with attractive odds and ends of antique china, that had come from the home of Matthew and Cornelia's parents.

They had both been doctors, working in partnership, and they had expected, from certain talents that their children had shown in their early years, that they would follow in their footsteps. But Matthew had taken the road into pure science and Cornelia, after changing her mind a number of times, had taken a degree in psychology and had just begun to work in a school for the mentally retarded when she had changed her mind once more and married Colin. She still occasionally did some voluntary work in a school for backward children in Godchester, though since she and Colin had bought the cottage in Fernley three years ago she had tended more and more to drop her other interests.

Colin was sitting writing at the table in the living room when Cornelia and Matthew came in, but, sweeping the papers aside, he made room for Cornelia to lay the table for lunch. It consisted of bread and cheese, some radishes and onions and a bottle of cheap Spanish wine. Afterwards Matthew unpacked his suitcase in the small spare bedroom, which had a sloping ceiling, beams in the walls and one window that looked far out to sea. There was a tossing of whitecaps on the grey waves that afternoon and the wind whistled shrilly in the chimney. Grey clouds chased each other raggedly across the sky. Matthew thought that it

would rain soon, but unless the rain was very heavy, he
would go for a walk at least to the bench on the cliff-top. He
had brought an anorak and some strong shoes and was not
dismayed by the thought of getting wet.

In fact, the rain held off. When Matthew and Colin presently set out together there was a tingling moisture in the air
that chilled their faces, but it was not enough to make
Matthew pull up the hood of his red quilted anorak. Both
he and Colin carried walking-sticks. Matthew always bor-
rowed the same one when he came to the cottage. It had
belonged to his father and was a malacca cane with a brass
ferule, a collar of silver on which his father's initials, J.K.T.,
were inscribed, and a handle of deer horn.

Taking it today out of the old-fashioned brass umbrella
stand in which the Naylors kept their collection of walking-
sticks, Matthew had said, "D'you know, I can remember
when I used to chew this handle, like a dog with a bone,
when I was a child?"

"Do you really?" Cornelia said. "How old were you
when you did a thing like that?"

"About three, I think."

"And you really remember it?"

"Clearly."

"Then you'd better keep it," she said with a laugh. "It
ought to have been yours anyway, as it's a man's stick. I
don't know how it came to me. Keep it and chew it again if
it still tastes good."

"Do you really mean that?"

"Of course I do. You're welcome."

"Then thanks."

It pleased him, as he swung the stick as he and Colin
walked along, that the stick was his, and he tried to think of
some present that he could give Cornelia in return. Perhaps

he could find something in the local antique shop, kept by Tim Welsh and his father, that would appeal to her.

He and Colin walked up the muddy lane in front of the houses to the point where it came to an end as it joined the cliff path that went back down the hill behind the houses to the village and also straight on for some miles until it dropped down to the next village in another fold of the downs. The bench at the point where the lane and the path joined was deserted today and looked wet and uninviting.

"Want to go on?" Colin asked.

"For a bit," Matthew answered.

They went on along the path, talking very little and Colin leaving it to Matthew to say when he wanted to turn back.

It was bleak and silent up on the cliffs, except for the mournful crying of sea-gulls and the grinding sound of the surf on the rocks below. Because of the low, dark clouds dusk came early and the chill in the air grew sharper.

"Let's go back," Matthew said at last. "It'll be dark soon."

"Just as you like." Colin walked with the long, easy strides of the athlete that he had once been and the climb up the cliff had not winded him at all, whereas Matthew had found his breathing labouring. "Some more of this sort of thing will do you good."

"Yes, it's what I need."

They turned back along the path towards the village.

They had just passed the bench when they saw two figures coming towards them. In the twilight Matthew took them at first for a man and a boy, then as they came nearer he saw that they were a man and a young girl. The man had an arm affectionately round the girl's shoulders. He was about Matthew's age. The girl could not have been more than twenty.

Seeing Colin and Matthew, they both paused and the man said in a friendly voice, "Hallo."

"Hallo, Grant," Colin answered. "Matthew, this is our neighbour, Grant Staveley. And his daughter, Eleanor. Grant, this is my brother-in-law, Matthew Tierney."

"Ah, the professor," Grant Staveley said. "Of course, I've heard about you from Colin and Cornelia. I'm sorry for your great misfortune."

His voice was pleasantly deep and resonant. Matthew was feeling bewildered. Without being quite aware of having done so, he had built up a picture in his mind of what Staveley would look like. He had imagined him a rather Mephistophelian figure, slender, elegant, with aquiline, mocking features and penetrating dark eyes. His hair would be thick and dark, growing low in a peak on his forehead, and it would not be surprising if a pair of horns should be found to be nestling in it. A conventional picture, of course, which Matthew did not take very seriously, but the reality was so different that for a moment he had the feeling that some deception was being practised upon him.

Grant Staveley was about his own height, but because he was far more heavily built, looked stocky. He had big feet, big hands and a big head, all without any elegance whatever. His face was large and mud-coloured, with features that looked as if they had been slapped on to it by an unskilful potter. They were rough, heavy and irregular. But it was an intelligent face and the eyes, which were light blue, looked uncommonly penetrating. He had thin, sandy hair which he wore almost to his shoulders and which the wind had blown into a tangle. He was dressed in ancient slacks, a black pullover with a polo neck and a green anorak, and he carried a walking-stick.

Seeing Matthew's, he held out his own and, speaking casually, as if they were in the middle of a conversation, remarked, "Almost identical. Mine belonged to my father. Yours belonged to yours, I expect. I've seen others like them, the silver band, the horn handle. A model in favour at one time with almost every Edwardian gentleman."

The girl put in, "I'm not his daughter, I'm his step-daughter and my name's Landon."

She had a rather gruff voice, something like a boy's when it is breaking, yet oddly attractive. She was tall, with narrow hips and wide shoulders and was wearing jeans and a leather jacket, so it was not altogether surprising that Matthew had taken her for a boy. Yet in spite of her boyishness, there was something intensely feminine about her, and something about the softness of her lips, her small, delicate features and her blue eyes that gave her face a blank look of childishness. She had very fair hair which was looped back from her face with a ribbon and fell almost to her waist.

"I knew your wife, of course," Staveley went on. "I painted her portrait. She told me you didn't like it."

He sounded as if he did not resent the fact in the least.

"It wasn't my idea of her," Matthew answered.

"I can't say for sure it was mine. Does it matter in the end if a portrait's in the least like the sitter? What do we know about the real faces of the people who sat to the great portrait painters? Their actual faces are all forgotten. It's the painting that counts. When I painted your wife it was just a portrait of a certain kind of woman that I wanted to paint. I'll take it back from you if you don't like it."

"I haven't decided what I want to do with it yet." Matthew knew that he wanted to get rid of the portrait, but he was fairly sure that he did not want it to go back to Grant Staveley, though he was very confused in his feelings about the man. He could not think what there had been about him to attract Kate. Certainly not his looks. But he gave off a sense of vitality that made Matthew feel uncomfortably desiccated. Had that been his charm? "But I'll bear your offer in mind," he added.

"Yes, do. Well, come along, child." The artist gave his stepdaughter a slap on her bottom. "Time we went home. Are you staying long, Professor?"

"I'm not sure," Matthew said.

"Well, we'll meet again soon, I expect. Good night."

Matthew and Colin both said good night and continued on down the path behind the house while Staveley and the girl turned off it into the lane.

"Well, what d'you think of him, now you've met him?" Colin asked. "Is he a man who'd make anonymous telephone calls?"

"It seems unlikely," Matthew admitted. "There's something too tough about him. Still, you never know. . . ." He broke off, standing still. They were just behind the white house in which Colin had told him in the Volunteer that Staveley lived. It was a long, low, pleasant-looking house, thatched like the Naylors', with a low wall surrounding the garden, with a gate in it that opened on to the path. But what had caught Matthew's attention was two borders filled with white flowers edging the narrow lawn that stretched from the house to the garden wall. At first, in the dusk, he could not make out what the flowers were, then he exclaimed, "White daffodils!"

"So they are," Colin agreed without much interest. "I prefer the yellow ones myself—seem more normal, somehow. It's yellow flowers that give you the feeling spring's really coming."

Matthew gave a slight shiver, not only because of the chill of the evening.

He muttered, "It doesn't feel much like spring today."

"Well, a drink will warm you up when we get in," Colin said. "Just about the right time for it. Come along."

They went on to the cottage.

Its door, as usual, was unlocked and Colin walked straight into the warm, bright living room with Matthew following him. A big log fire was burning in the grate. Bottles and glasses were on a tray on the table. Cornelia was sitting at the telephone. She was just putting it down as the two men came in and she looked round at them with a stunned look of shock on her face.

"She telephoned!" she breathed in a hoarse whisper, as if she could hardly get the words out. "She spoke to me. She said, 'How much of the loot did you and your husband get for that alibi?' Then she didn't wait for an answer. She just rang off. Oh, it was horrible!"

CHAPTER FOUR

Colin went to the tray of drinks, poured out a large whisky and took it to Cornelia. She reached out for it with both hands, but they were shaking so much that some of the whisky slopped out of the glass. Colin took it from her and held it to her mouth. She spluttered as she swallowed, then drew a deep breath and thrust Colin's hand and the glass away from her.

"I'm sorry, this isn't like me, is it?" she said. "I don't know why I'm so upset." Her voice quavered a little. "But I know how you felt, Matthew, when you got those calls."

"You said 'she,'" he said. "Are you sure it was a woman's voice? My impression was that it was a man's."

She looked bewildered. "I said 'she,' did I? Yes, I think it was a woman's. But perhaps it could have been a man's. I don't really know. I was taken so by surprise, I didn't really have time to think."

Matthew unzipped his anorak and dropped it on to a chair. He poured out whisky for himself.

"That's how it was with me the first time," he said. "The second time I thought it was a man, talking falsetto."

Cornelia's trembling had stopped. She reached for the glass that Colin was holding and sipped from it, frowning.

"That's what it could have been, I suppose," she said. "Someone disguising his voice. Which means that it could be someone we know. In fact, it probably is. And that's why I went to bits in that stupid way. I think it was the feeling that it's someone we know here who hates us. I didn't know there was anybody who hated us, but there must be someone who does."

"I don't think you need to be too sure of that," Matthew said. He sat down in one of the wicker chairs, near to the cheerfully crackling fire. "You may come into it only incidentally. I may still be the target."

"But in that case it would have to be someone who knows you're here with us and that means just a few of our friends."

"I agree that's probable."

"You asked me yourself who knew about Colin giving you that alibi for lunch-time," Cornelia said. "And I told you Tim Welsh knew and I suppose he could have told anyone, but it would have to be someone in Fernley."

"But you haven't told me of anyone in Fernley, except Staveley, who got enough involved with Kate when she was staying with you here to feel impelled to do a thing like this." Perhaps it was partly the whisky and the warmth of the pleasant room after the cold outside, but it seemed to Matthew that he was thinking unusually clearly. "It happens that Colin and I met Staveley out on the cliff this evening. When we separated he'd have had time to get home and make that call just before we got in."

"You've got Grant on the brain," Colin said, pouring out some whisky for himself and sitting down on the arm of Cornelia's chair and putting an arm round her shoulders. The wind had whipped colour into his cheeks and ruffled his dark, curly hair. "I believe you half-believe he murdered Kate, but you haven't even hinted at a motive. D'you think he's some kind of sex maniac?"

"More surprising things than that have come to light," Matthew said. "But suppose it was just that Kate had some kind of hold over him. If they'd been lovers, for instance, and she was threatening to tell his wife, perhaps trying to make him leave her, wouldn't that have been a motive?"

"Not for Grant," Colin said. "That marriage has survived worse episodes than Kate. Rachel's a woman of enormous patience."

"What's their financial situation?" Matthew asked. "Is he dependent on her, by any chance?"

"Not to my knowledge," Colin said. "She runs a shop in Fernley, a sort of souvenir place that relies mainly on selling holiday knick-knacks to tourists in the summer. I shouldn't think it's ever made much money. I think she keeps it going mostly to have something to do."

"All right, let's forget about him as the murderer for the moment," Matthew said. "Isn't he still the likeliest person to have made those telephone calls?"

"Why?"

"Because he knew Kate. He may even have been fond of her in a way. And he's a violent type, I should think. That's my impression of him. And he may have been utterly outraged at her murder and felt that he'd got to do something about it. He may quite sincerely think I'm guilty. We don't know what kind of things Kate may have told him about me. And if I'm guilty, that means my alibi must be a fake, which you and I have cooked up together. He knew about it because of what you probably told him on the train, and what he's trying to do at the moment is to intimidate you or me into breaking down."

"Damn-fool thing to try," Colin remarked. He was stroking Cornelia's shoulder. "What d'you think about this, love? You're being very quiet."

"Oh, I think it's some lunatic who got the story of the alibi from Tim," she answered. She had regained her self-control and was sitting relaxed in the crook of Colin's arm. "Someone who's only doing it to annoy. Probably he doesn't care a pin about Kate's murder, but pestering us gives him a lot of pleasure. My idea that it must be someone who hates us was a bit exaggerated. It's funny, though, isn't it, what a frightening thing the thought of hatred like that can be? Even when you know the person can't harm you. But I'm still sure it's someone we know."

"How many lunatics do we know, give or take a few?" Colin asked. "A round dozen, maybe."

"Oh, don't be silly." She held out her glass to him. "Give me some more of that, then I'll go and get us something to eat." As he got up to refill her glass, she went on, "The sort of lunatic I'm talking about wouldn't be recognisable. He— or she, if I was right about the voice in the first place—is probably some highly respected member of the community and may even be coming for drinks here tomorrow. I didn't tell you about that, did I? When our caller rang up, I'd just been phoning round a few people to ask them in for drinks around six tomorrow, and I was still thinking about that, standing right there beside the telephone and wondering if I'd ring up anybody else, when it rang and startled me and I heard this voice, and the sheer shock of it made me lose my head and panic."

"Drinks tomorrow?" Matthew said. "You're giving a party tomorrow? You aren't expecting me to be there, are you?"

"Of course I am," she said. "I did it on your account. As I told you this morning, you've got to meet people, not go into hiding. And it's only a few people whom you're bound to meet sometime anyway—Grant and Rachel and Eleanor, and the Welshes, and a couple called Richardson who've just retired here and don't know many people yet, and Dr. Parkes, who'll come if he's free. That's all."

"Well, count me out," Matthew said. "I'll go for a walk."

"You will not," Cornelia said.

"Or I'll read upstairs."

"Matthew, my dear," she said patiently, "do believe me, I understand how you feel, but all the same you'll come to our party and afterwards you'll say I was right to insist. The more normally you live, the better you'll feel for it. Hiding yourself isn't going to do you any good at all. And they're all very nice people. They won't be tactless or inquisitive."

"Always remembering," Colin said with a grin, "that one of them is probably a raving lunatic. And who knows, Matthew, if you come, you may even recognise a voice."

An argument that had more influence with Matthew than Cornelia's concern for his good. Muttering that he thought he had been promised peace and quiet, he resigned himself to facing the party next day.

The guests began to arrive soon after six o'clock. Matthew had only just got in from a walk that he had taken by himself along the cliff path. All day it had been still and mild, not blustery as it had been the day before. It was one of the days when there is the softness of spring in the air, a gentleness that promises that winter is at last letting go its clutch on the earth. The surf pounded as hard as ever at the foot of the cliffs, but out to sea the water was smooth and silken. Tomorrow might be as fierce a day as yesterday, but for the moment there was a calm that gave Matthew a surprising sense of calm in himself. Breathing in deeply the tang of the sea, he walked steadily on, swinging his horn-handled stick and thinking of nothing at all. A pity that he had promised to return for the party, but Cornelia meant well. He was still in his room, putting on a tie and combing his hair, when he heard the front door open and her voice raised in greeting.

The first arrivals were Tim Welsh and his father, Ambrose, the antique dealer. Cornelia introduced them to Matthew while Colin poured out drinks. Tim Welsh was a very tall, well-built young man, with a longish, mild, good-natured face, curly brown hair, brown eyes and a pleasantly smiling mouth. Matthew, accustomed to making swift assessments of the potentialities of the young, rated him as not highly intelligent or imaginative, but probably reliable and hardworking and very honest. He noticed the boy's strong, sensitive, craftsman's hands and remembered how pleased Cornelia had been with the work that he had done on her Georgian tallboy. She had also insisted that Tim was very normal and would never have made anonymous telephone calls, and on seeing him Matthew felt ready to believe that she was right.

His father was harder to place. Ambrose Welsh was several inches shorter than his son and so light in build as to be almost birdlike. Yet there was a look of muscular agility about him, a quickness of movement that made him look as if he were made of tough wire springs. His face was long, like his son's, but was also very narrow, with a sharp, jutting nose, a tight mouth and singularly bright, dark eyes under finely arched dark eyebrows. It was the kind of face that might have been very handsome when he was young, but now was spoilt by a look of nervous petulance. His hair was already white and had receded from his high forehead, leaving it with the smooth, polished look of bone. Matthew wondered how well the father and son understood one another. The boy gave an impression of easy-going tolerance, but Ambrose Welsh did not look like a man with whom it would be particularly easy to get along.

However, his approach to Matthew was friendly.

"I saw you out walking on the cliffs this afternoon," he said. "Sensible to take advantage of weather like today's. Tim was looking after the shop for me and I was putting in a little time gardening, getting the roses pruned. We live next door—did Cornelia tell you that? In the grey house be-

tween this and the Staveleys'. The house belongs to the
Staveleys, as a matter of fact. It's part of the property they
bought last year when they moved in here. I think they
thought they could get Tim and me out quite easily, demol-
ish the house and develop the site. It could be a little gold
mine, the way this part of the coast has been getting more
and more popular year by year. But luckily the sitting ten-
ant has his rights. Naturally they offered to compensate us
for moving, but we've lived in that house for ten years and
nobody's going to get us out."

"Now, Ambrose, you don't have to get started on that,"
Cornelia said. "The Staveleys are coming this evening and
we don't want to spend the time arguing about your house.
We all know no one can make you move out if you don't
want to, and I'm very glad too, because it would ruin things
for us if some fearful monstrosity got built next door."

"Ah, you never know what may happen," Ambrose Welsh
replied. "Staveley's been working like a mole in the dark
with some members of the council. I happen to know it. So
if Tim and I are out in the street one day, don't be surprised. But I'll go on fighting while there's any fight left
in me."

"Dad, that's slanderous," Tim Welsh said. "It's accusing
members of the council of bribery and corruption. You'd
better watch it."

"But bribery and corruption is what it is!" his father
cried. "Isn't it, Cornelia? Colin, don't you agree with me?
Isn't it a scandal?"

Colin had handed drinks all round.

"Don't worry, you'll still be in that house when Cornelia
and I are underground," he said. "The law's all on the ten-
ant's side these days."

"But Staveley's very cunning, you know," Welsh went on.
"All that bluff, hearty act of his, it's all fake, absolute fake.

When it's anything to do with money he's got the mind of a weasel—" He stopped himself with a little titter. "Sorry, Cornelia, he's a friend of yours, of course. Please forgive me. I won't say a word about the house when he gets here."

"I think he's completely given up the idea of getting you out," Cornelia said. "It's you who won't give up your lovely fight with him." She did not sound perturbed. The subject was apparently so familiar that it was not of consequence any longer. "Now behave yourself properly, Ambrose, because here are the Richardsons, and they're newcomers and we want them to think we're nice people, and they may not understand your line in party small talk."

She went to open the door, letting in a breath of cool evening air and two small, elderly people with smoothly brushed grey hair, grey clothes and anxious, diffidently smiling faces.

Somehow they cornered Matthew and seemed to cling to him as if they were afraid of everyone else in the room. They told him a great deal about themselves, of which he later remembered almost nothing, except that Mr. Richardson had been a headmaster in a comprehensive school and Mrs. Richardson a physiotherapist and that they had a granddaughter at Sussex University who was studying social anthropology. They seemed to take for granted that this would be a matter of great interest to Matthew and he did his best to act as if it were, although the only important thing that registered with him about the Richardsons was that it was inconceivable that either of them could be his anonymous caller. All the time that they were talking to him he tried to listen to Ambrose Welsh talking to Cornelia, to listen for anything in the man's voice that might remind him of that impersonal, falsetto voice that he had heard on the telephone, but the shy little voices of the Richardsons distracted him, even though he had lost the thread of what they were saying.

"Such a lovely girl!" Mrs. Richardson suddenly exclaimed, and Matthew was never clear in his mind whether she was referring to her granddaughter at Sussex, or to Eleanor Landon, who had just come into the room, followed by her mother and stepfather.

Out on the cliffs it had not occurred to Matthew that Eleanor was lovely, but now he found that he had to think again. She had twisted up her long, pale hair into a coil at the back of her head, drawing it so severely back from her face that it showed up its beautiful bones. She was wearing a good deal of make-up, which added several years to her age, while emphasising a challenging quality in her femininity. In a long, high-waisted dress of clinging silk jersey she had entirely lost the look of boyishness that had gone with her jacket and jeans. As she came into the room her eyes lit up brilliantly and it was obvious at once whom the brilliance was for. She had seen Tim Welsh, and as he smiled across the room at her, she gave only the briefest of absent-minded greetings to Colin and Cornelia, went straight to Tim and stood close to him, gazing up into his face.

As she did this, Matthew caught sight of Grant Staveley's face and was startled by the way it tightened with anger. Staveley looked both enraged and baffled by what he saw, as if he could hardly stop himself protesting at it and yet knew that he must hold himself in. Matthew did not like his expression and turned his head to look with some curiosity at Rachel Staveley.

She was a pale, quiet-looking woman of about forty, with the same good bones as her daughter, though she was built on an altogether smaller scale. Her hair, as fair as Eleanor's, was cut short and had a soft, smooth wave in it. She was wearing a dark red trouser suit which looked as if it had once been good but had had a fairly long life. She kissed both Colin and Cornelia, took a glass of sherry from Colin and, on being introduced to Matthew, gave him a grave smile, seemed to search his face swiftly for something which, it might have been, she almost feared to find there, then turned to Ambrose Welsh.

Did she think, then, that Matthew was a murderer, he wondered. Had she been expecting to find it written on his face?

She said to Welsh, "We're meeting on neutral ground this evening, aren't we, Ambrose? I hope we aren't going to quarrel."

She had a low, calm voice without much expression.

"I never quarrel with you, Rachel," he answered. "I reserve my fire for that mad husband of yours."

Staveley laughed. "Sometimes I wonder whom you reserved it for before we came to live here," he said. "Whom did you quarrel with before we moved in? Not our predecessor. You couldn't possibly have quarrelled with that dear old woman."

"Certainly not," Welsh said. "I had the greatest regard for Miss Appleby. As a landlord she had the very good sense to leave us in peace. I used to mow her grass and prune her shrubs. We got on excellently."

"Colin, who was Ambrose's enemy before we came to live here?" Staveley asked. "He can't possibly have got on without one."

"I think it was a certain Income Tax Inspector," Colin replied. "Ambrose used to write him abusive postcards with double meanings, hoping they'd get read by everyone in the man's office. He used to come and show them to us before he posted them to see if we didn't think them witty. Some of them were."

"Did he sign them?" Staveley asked.

"*Sign* them?" Welsh cried. "Of course I signed them. What would have been the point of sending them if the bloody rat hadn't known where they came from? Would you think I'm the kind of nutter who writes anonymous letters?"

There was a sudden silence. It could have happened by chance, as it can in any group of people. It could have been that the rising excitement in Welsh's voice embarrassed the others. But one person turned and looked directly at Matthew at that moment. It was Rachel Staveley.

In the silence there was a knock at the door and Colin, going to answer it, welcomed in a tall, slight man in his early fifties, with thick, untidy grey hair, horn-rimmed spectacles and an amiable, harassed face. He introduced him to Matthew as Dr. Parkes. The doctor gave Matthew one of those searching, rather wary glances to which he was becoming accustomed, murmured a greeting, then seemed very ready to leave him to the Richardsons, who went eagerly back to discussing the merits of the newer universities compared with Oxford and Cambridge. They at least were neither wary nor watchful in their attitude to him, which made him far more grateful for their company than he had been at first and more attentive to what they had to tell him of the problems of their granddaughter.

Then in another silence that happened a few minutes later, Cornelia said, "Talking of anonymous letters—Matthew has been receiving anonymous telephone calls. So have we, as a matter of fact. We had one yesterday evening."

She said it deliberately and then deliberately looked round from face to face in the room.

Matthew realised that she had planned to do this all along and had only been waiting for the right moment, but he saw astonishment on Colin's face, then a firm closing of

his lips, as if he were holding back what he felt inclined to
say. So she had not taken him into her confidence about
what she intended to do. Matthew for an instant felt blind
rage, then a kind of helplessness, a type of response that he
had had off and on throughout his life to actions of Cornelia's. He gave a slight sigh and said nothing.

The first to speak was Rachel Staveley. In the level voice
that did not sound capable of surprise, she said, "How very
unpleasant. You've told the police, I suppose."

"No, as a matter of fact, we haven't," Cornelia said.
"What can they do?"

"But what were the calls about?" Eleanor asked. "Were
they obscene or what?"

"Not obscene, no," Cornelia said. "But threatening, in a
way. I'm inclined to think it's just some crank, trying to
frighten us. But Matthew thinks it's someone beginning to
try to soften us up for blackmail. Only the blackmailer's got
hold of the wrong end of the stick. He—or she—Matthew
thought it was a man and I thought it was a woman—seems
to believe that Matthew's paid Colin some huge sum to say
they had lunch together on the day Kate was murdered.
And of course, if it were true, it would mean that Matthew
was Kate's murderer, otherwise he wouldn't need the alibi.
But it happens that Matthew and Colin did have lunch together that day, and Matthew's time was completely filled
up for the rest of the day as well and he can prove it all, so
this character who's annoying us with his telephone calls is
simply wasting his time. He can keep on and on with it and
it will get him precisely nowhere."

"And just why," Staveley demanded with another flash of
anger, "have you chosen to tell us all this at this moment?
You've done it for some reason, haven't you, Cornelia? You
never do anything without a reason. You think one of us
here is your caller and you're tipping him off it's no good."

"Why ever should you think I'd do a thing like that?" Cornelia asked innocently. "It just happened to come into my mind, that's all. As a matter of fact, it's been on my mind ever since I took the call last night. I couldn't stop myself speaking about it."

"Your brother doesn't look as if he's grateful to you for it," Staveley said sardonically. "Well, Tierney, which of us strikes you as most likely to be your blackmailer? Am I guilty?"

"Of course, of course!" Welsh said with one of his titters. "I thought of you immediately. It's perfectly in character for you to work in the dark."

"Now, please, please," little Mrs. Richardson said, "don't embarrass poor Professor Tierney. He's been through enough already. Of course no one here would dream of doing anything so nasty. You know, dear Mrs. Naylor, ever since Norman and I came to live here we've been saying how wonderfully lucky we are to find ourselves in such a really nice community. So many interesting people and all so friendly. . . ."

She talked on gently and inexorably till no one could quite remember what they had been nearly quarrelling about.

Matthew felt so grateful to her that he hoped her granddaughter would get a brilliant First and would then obtain all the grants she wanted to take her to whatever far parts of the earth she required to visit in the course of her career. Yet as Mrs. Richardson talked on, it seemed to him that everyone else in the room had started to look at him with even more concentration than before. Particularly he noticed the way that the doctor looked at him, as if Matthew were a patient of his whom he suspected of trying to conceal from him the symptoms of a mortal illness.

Presently Dr. Parkes said to Cornelia, "You said that you

answered a telephone call from this man, didn't you? You didn't simply hear a voice you didn't know ask for Professor Tierney and hand the phone over to him?"

So the man thought the calls might be an invention, did he, Matthew thought. An invention deliberately made up for some obscure purpose.

"I heard the whole call myself," Cornelia answered. "In fact, Matthew and Colin were out of the house when it came." She shook her head at the doctor. "No one's made up this story. It's only too unpleasantly real."

"No, well, I just wondered. . . ." Dr. Parkes said vaguely.

Shortly afterwards he took his leave and the others soon followed, leaving behind the feeling of lifelessness that descends on a house when a number of guests have just left it. The bright, pleasant room seemed suddenly to become unnaturally silent, as well as disordered, with empty glasses here and there and ash-trays overflowing and cushions flattened. Cornelia went quietly round the room, collecting the glasses and taking them out to the kitchen, plumping up the cushions and emptying the ash-trays into the fire.

She was planting another log in the grate when Colin exclaimed, "What a perfectly bloody party! What in hell were you thinking of, Cornelia, getting that gang of people together? They all hate each other."

"I wanted Matthew to see the Staveleys and the Welshes in action," she answered. "Of course, Parkes and the Richardsons were just camouflage. I couldn't ask the others here by themselves, could I? They'd have thought I'd gone mad."

"I don't think any of them liked me much," Matthew said. "They gave me some very peculiar glances."

"It's one another they don't like," she said. "You've nothing to worry about."

"And then dragging in those telephone calls!" Colin exclaimed. "And the way you looked round when you'd done it! You were as good as accusing someone in the room of having made them."

"It won't hurt anyone in the room who isn't guilty," she said calmly. "And if one of them is, it may have discouraged him. Those calls are a nuisance, if they're nothing worse."

"Anyway, why just the Staveleys and the Welshes?" Colin asked. "Why didn't you ask the whole of Fernley?"

"They were the people Kate saw most of while she was staying with us," Cornelia said. "In fact, she didn't really see anything of anyone else. So they seemed the most likely people to feel enough involved with her to be interfering and trying to make trouble for us now." She turned to Matthew. "What did you make of them, Matthew?"

He had been sitting on one of the wicker chairs, staring at nothing. His anger with Cornelia had subsided but had left him with a sense of depressing lassitude. His fits of anger, notably those that he had bottled up, often had that effect upon him. He was wondering why he had ever come to Fernley. He was unlikely to find the peace and quiet he had wanted as long as Cornelia insisted on taking charge of his life.

He gave a slight start. "Sorry—what were you saying?"

"I asked what you made of the Welshes and the Staveleys," she said.

"Oh, I don't know," he said indifferently. "Welsh is a peculiar character. What happened to his wife?"

"She died of a stomach cancer about ten years ago," Cornelia answered. "He's said to have been devoted to her. Anyway, he's never married again. But there've been other women along the way, I believe. Rumour has it that Rachel Landon, as she was then, was one of them, and her marrying Grant is the real reason for the quarrel between the families."

"How long ago did she marry Staveley?" Matthew asked.

"About six or seven years. It was before we got the cottage. When we first met them they were living in the flat above her shop."

"The Landon girl and the Welsh boy don't seem to want to keep the quarrel going."

"Ah no, they're quite wonderfully in love, aren't they?" Cornelia laughed. "But they're so young, I dare say nothing'll come of it. Now I'd better get us something to eat. Will omelets do? I don't feel like bothering with anything else."

She disappeared into the kitchen.

Colin and Matthew remained sitting silent in the living room, Colin close to the fire, leaning forward with its flickering lighting up answering glints in his dark eyes and deepening the ruddy colour of his face, while Matthew leant back in his chair, gazing vacantly into space.

Colin was frowning as if he had some difficult and harassing problem on his mind. Matthew was idly wondering if it would be a good idea to return to London tomorrow and at the same time trying to remember if any of the voices that he had heard that evening in the room reminded him of the voice that he had heard on the telephone. But nothing came of the effort. Probably, he thought, he would never know for certain who the caller had been, for Cornelia's crude tactics would very likely turn out to have frightened him off. And no doubt in time Matthew would feel grateful for it.

He did not return to London the next day. After a restless night, he ended up oversleeping, then spent most of the day lying on his bed, reading. Then in the late afternoon he went for his usual walk along the cliff path. The feeling of spring of the day before had gone and winter was back once more, though the air was not particularly cold. But it was a bleak day, with the greyness of the sky merging at the horizon with the greyness of the waves and flecks of white dotting the drab expanse of the sea. Matthew walked almost as far as the next village and, turning back, sat for some time on the lonely bench near the Staveleys' house, until he realised that he was beginning to get cold, when he got up and continued towards the cottage.

He had been trying to focus his mind on the future, which in a way was an attempt to analyse what his feelings had been about Kate. For what would make the future different from the past was of course the simple fact that she would not be there. He was in one of his dark moods, in which he almost believed that it should have been possible for him to have prevented her death. What that meant, he knew, was that he was having an attack of feeling that he had not loved her enough. But surely that had been her fault as much as his. Neither of them had been happy in their marriage. But there had been something once, at least on his side. He was not sure that she had ever loved him much, even at the beginning. It had sometimes seemed to him that what she had wanted had simply been to get married to a man who already had an established career, who could give her a comfortable and protected life. She had been very insecure as a young woman, very much in need of a helping hand. That had been before her legacy, of course. If it had come sooner, perhaps she would never have married him.

And now the money was his. . . .

As he thought of that, he gave an abrupt shudder. Pain surged into his mind, defeating his attempt at detachment. It seemed deeply wrong to have gained so much from someone who had been so little a part of him.

"Good evening, Professor," a voice said from behind the garden wall that he was passing.

Ambrose Welsh was at his garden gate. He was in a thick sweater, corduroy trousers and Wellington boots and was holding a pair of secateurs.

"You looked very deep in thought," he said. "I'm afraid I've interrupted you."

"Not at all," Matthew replied automatically. "You've been busy in your garden?"

"Yes, finishing the roses. Tim's a splendidly hardworking boy, but only when it's something to do with furniture. He's a true craftsman, far more skilled than I am, though I taught him the job. But I've never been able to persuade him to touch the garden. By the way, I think I ought to apologise for yesterday."

"For what? It was a very pleasant evening," Matthew lied.

"We were very discourteous to you, letting our private quarrels come out into the open like that in the presence of a stranger." Welsh smoothed a lock of his white hair back from his bony forehead. He did not look at all apologetic, but rather pleased with himself. "It's a sad fact, however, that Staveley and I can hardly speak to one another without sparks flying. It really isn't my fault. I'm not at all a quarrelsome man. They were just joking about that, as I hope you realised. But Staveley can't stand it if he isn't the centre of attention, particularly if there's an attractive woman about. I remember it with your wife, you know. A very attractive woman, very. It's sad to think about it now and perhaps it's bad taste on my part even to mention it, but he really did his best to captivate her. I used to laugh about it, it was so blatant."

"And did he?" Matthew's mouth felt dry.

"Did he what?"

"Captivate her, as you put it?"

"Ah, how can you tell with a woman like that? She'd never make a parade of her feelings."

"What were Staveley's feelings about her, then?"

"Lord bless you, Staveley's never had any feelings for anyone except that stepdaughter of his. He's crazy about her. I don't know how Rachel puts up with it. A quite unnatural situation, incestuous almost, although he and the girl aren't actually blood relations. But there's something abnormal about it. He's very possessive, won't let any other man come near her, completely dominates her. She and my son are very attracted to one another, but Staveley's doing his best to ruin it for them, tells her she's too young, that Tim isn't good enough for her, that he's just a clod she'll soon get tired of. I remember discussing it all with your wife. She'd noticed it before I said anything about it. A very intelligent woman. She said to me—"

"Good night," Matthew interrupted loudly and abruptly strode off down the path towards the cottage. He was not sure what he might have done if he had stayed there any longer, listening to Ambrose Welsh talking about Kate.

CHAPTER FIVE

When Matthew entered the cottage he found Colin sitting at the table, writing, with papers spread out around him. He was a compulsive writer of notes to scientific journals, though the work seldom went much further. Cornelia was sitting by the fire, knitting. A savoury smell of something in a casserole came from the kitchen.

Matthew thrust his walking-stick into the stand and sat down facing Cornelia across the hearth.

"I've just been talking to your friend Welsh," he said. "I don't like him."

Colin bundled his papers together.

"One has to make the best of one's neighbours," he said. "Anyway, he isn't as bad as all that. He doesn't mean half the things he says."

"When it comes to practical things," Cornelia said, "he can be extraordinarily kind. He keeps an eye on the cottage for us when we're away and sometimes actually tidies up the garden, and once, when the two of us went down with flu at the same time, he did our shopping for us and brought in things he'd specially cooked for us, pies and stews and things. He's a very good cook."

"I don't like him," Matthew repeated. "I don't trust a word he says." After a moment he added, "I think I'll go to London tomorrow."

"London?" Cornelia exclaimed. "Not to stay! You aren't going back to that terrible house!"

"No, I thought I'd just go up for the day, if that's all right with you," he said. "I thought I'd look in on that man Mellish, to see if they've got anywhere at all, and perhaps look in at the department to see if anything's come up I ought to attend to."

"I see." She finished the row that she was knitting. "Matthew, I'm sorry about that party. Colin's been lecturing me about it. I thought it was a good idea, but you hated it, didn't you? But I meant well, I really did."

Matthew smiled. It was a feat to have wrung an apology from Cornelia.

"You always do," he said.

"I saw Rachel this morning," she went on, "and she said you seemed awfully depressed, and that she knew from her own experience when her first husband died that parties and meeting strangers were the last things she'd been able to face. She rather went for me about it. I've been an awful fool. Truly, I'm sorry."

"It doesn't matter," Matthew said. "Who was her first husband?"

"An air-line pilot. He was killed in a crash. They were still quite young, only in their twenties, I think. Eleanor was just an infant. You know, sometimes I think she was the real reason Rachel married Grant. She wanted Eleanor to have a father. And he's always been very fond of her and very good to her. I think that may be why Rachel puts up with as much from him as she does. She feels that in his way he's fulfilling his side of their bargain."

Matthew thought how different this sounded from what Ambrose Welsh had said about the relationship between Staveley and his stepdaughter. But which version was the truth? Was Cornelia very naïve, or was Welsh simply evil-minded? Or had each got hold of a portion of the truth? And what had it to do with him? He yawned. The warmth of the room after his walk was making him drowsy. If Colin had not got up then and made drinks for the three of them Matthew would probably have gone quietly to sleep in his comfortable chair.

Next morning he took the eight-three to London. The first thing he did when he arrived at Waterloo was to take the Underground train to Golders Green and walk up the long road to his house. He was uncertain why he felt that he had to do this. Until he had arrived at Waterloo he had not even intended it, yet his steps had taken him straight to the Underground station and he had found himself making his way home.

Not that it felt in the least like home when he let himself in at the front door. The house had the feeling, the smell, the chill, of a place that has been empty for months. Of course, that was only his imagination. He had been gone for less than a week. But as he roamed through the rooms, seeing the dust that had settled on the furniture, he had an eerie feeling of being a stranger in the place. After all, something far more dramatic, more astounding and shattering had happened here while he had been out of it than anything that he himself had ever experienced. It seemed to exclude him. Nervously he forced himself to go into the sitting room and found himself face to face with Grant Staveley's portrait of Kate.

He hated it even more than before and felt more puzzled than ever how Kate could ever have been as pleased with it as she had seemed to be. Had she been so infatuated with the man that anything that he had done had seemed to her precious and that she could not see its cruelty?

Matthew left the room quickly, let himself out of the house and set off for the police station.

He did not know what hope there was of finding Mellish available, and if he was not, whether or not some subordinate would be able to talk to him about the case. However, after only a short wait, he was shown into Mellish's office. The big man stood up behind his desk, holding out a hand. His big, square face with its oddly small features was blandly impersonal. He said that he was glad to see Matthew, gestured him to a chair and offered him a cigarette.

When Matthew shook his head, Mellish lit one for himself and, when he had inhaled deeply, remarked, "Wise man. I keep giving it up every few months, hold out for a week or two, then think I can trust myself to have an odd one or two with a cup of coffee and there I am, straight off, smoking fifty a day as before. No strength of will, that's my trouble."

Matthew was sure that whatever the Superintendent's trouble in life might be, it was not a lack of strength of will.

"Of course you know why I've come," Matthew said.

"Yes, you want to know if we've made any progress. Very natural." Mellish leant back in his chair, puffing a haze of smoke towards Matthew. "Well, we haven't got far, I'm afraid, but something's come up I wanted to talk to you about, so I'm very glad you've come in. We found a bracelet which corresponds to a description you gave us of one that belonged to your wife. I'd like you to look at it and see if you can identify it."

"So you still believe in your burglar, do you?" Matthew said.

"You don't?" Mellish asked.

"I never have."

"Because he didn't take the diamond ring? But that's the kind of thing people do in situations like that. Perhaps they simply lose their heads when they've killed someone when they'd never planned to do it, or some noise frightens them —the telephone, anything—and they run for it before they've had time to think what they're doing. And now we've got this bracelet, and if it belonged to your wife, it looks as if we may have been right about our burglar, doesn't it?"

Mellish opened a drawer in his desk, reached into it and brought out something in a plastic envelope. He opened the envelope and slid out of it on to the desk in front of Matthew a bracelet which he recognised immediately. It was of next to no value, but it was a pretty thing, made of silver and malachite, and it was one of the first presents that he had ever given Kate.

"Yes," he said after a moment, "it's hers."

"Go on, pick it up, make sure," Mellish said. "It's been tested for fingerprints and there are none on it except the pawnbroker's."

Matthew picked it up, pretended to look at it more carefully, though this was unnecessary, and put it down again.

"It's hers," he repeated. "Where did you find it?"

Mellish returned the bracelet to its envelope.

"There's a pawnbroker in Fulham called Eckert," he said. "When our list of stolen property got round to him he recognised the bracelet and notified us."

"Who took it to him?"

"A young girl. Age about eighteen. Small, dark. Gave the name of Bradshaw, almost certainly false. He didn't remember much about her except that she was dressed in jeans and some sort of leather jacket, as they all are nowadays, and she had what he thought was a North Country accent—Yorkshire or Lancashire, he wasn't sure which. Does that mean anything to you?"

Matthew shook his head.

"Tell me," he said, "a girl like that couldn't have murdered my wife, could she? It wouldn't have been physically possible. Kate was quite a strong woman."

He suddenly found that Mellish's small eyes, under their

shaggy, sandy eyebrows, were boring into his in the way which once before had given him the feeling that Mellish could look right into his skull, could intrude unforgivably.

"It might not have been absolutely impossible," Mellish said. "Unlikely, all the same. Women commit far fewer crimes of violence than men. When they take to murder, poison's their weapon. Or they get a man to do the job for them. But this girl could certainly be an accomplice of the murderer. His wife or girl friend or even his daughter, realising what she could on the jewellery for him. If she goes on doing it, we'll soon trace her and that'll take us straight to him. Don't worry, Professor, we'll get him sooner or later. Finding this bracelet was a break-through."

It sounded as if he meant it to be the end of the conversation, but Matthew did not move. He sat with his fingertips together, still looking at the bracelet on the desk, mistily green inside the plastic envelope.

"Yes," he said. "Yes, of course. But there are one or two things. . . ."

As he did not go on, Mellish began to tap impatiently with two fingers on his desk.

Matthew suddenly raised his eyes to the other man's.

"Suppose the murderer wasn't a burglar. Suppose he only took the jewellery to mislead us. Suppose the girl took the bracelet to the pawnbroker on purpose for it to be traced, so that you should feel quite sure you'd a burglar to look for."

"Subtle!" Mellish said. He made it sound as if in his vocabulary that was not a compliment.

"There are two things I haven't told you anything about, though perhaps I should have," Matthew went on. "One is that before I went down to stay with my sister and brother-in-law I had three telephone calls. I didn't recognise the voice of the caller and all he did was ask me how much I'd paid my brother-in-law for my alibi on the day of my wife's murder. When I asked him what he meant, he rang off. Then after I got to Fernley my sister had a call of the same kind. She thought hers was made by a woman, I thought mine was made by a man, but neither of us is sure. What I'm wondering now, since you told me about the girl who had the bracelet, could a man and a woman have been working together about those calls?"

Mellish's two fingers went on tapping on the desk.

"Why didn't you tell me anything about this before?"

"I didn't see the point. You couldn't possibly have traced the caller, could you?"

"All the same, I see now why you don't believe in our burglar. Whoever called you knew about that lunch you claimed to have had with Mr. Naylor and that means someone in your own circle. But it's hardly likely the caller and the murderer are the same person, is it? The murderer can still be the burglar, while the caller's someone who believes you murdered your wife. Someone who may be getting around to blackmail. Only you don't have to worry about that, do you, because we know quite well that you and Mr. Naylor did have lunch together."

"I was going to ask you about that," Matthew said. "Are you sure about it?"

"Oh yes, the barman at the Volunteer remembered you both quite clearly."

"That's good." Matthew was astonished at the relief that he felt. "Then there's the other thing. . . ."

"Yes?"

"It's difficult to talk about it. You asked me something about it when I saw you last and I couldn't bring myself to talk about it at all. Had my wife had a lover, you asked. Well, it's probable, I think, that she was involved somehow with a man in Fernley, an artist, Grant Staveley, who painted her portrait when she was down there in December, recuperating after an attack of flu. But I know very little about it. I don't know how far it went, or even if it went anywhere at all except in her imagination. All the same, there was something. . . . I'm fairly sure she was to some extent in love with him, but even that's based on something that may strike you as ridiculous. You see, after that visit to Fernley she developed a passion for white flowers. She wouldn't have any others in the house. And Staveley seems to have the same aberration. At the moment his garden's full of white daffodils. There isn't a yellow one in sight. And that's given me this feeling I have that he'd some kind of ascendancy over her. In other words, that she'd fallen in love with him, though I don't know anything about his feelings for her. Perhaps he hadn't any. And that may have made her suffer a great deal. In the last weeks of her life she was a very unhappy woman, that's something I'm sure of."

Mellish frowned. "There was a bunch of white narcissi in your sitting room when we found the body."

"I've been wondering about that," Matthew said. "Staveley was in London that day. Could he have brought them to her?"

"No," Mellish said. "She bought them herself in a shop called Singer's, a florist near the Golders Green Underground. The only important thing about that is that she went into the shop about ten-fifteen and that the flowers were the last of her purchases, so allowing her about a quarter of an hour to get home after she'd bought them, she was alive until at least ten-thirty. Probably longer, because there's the tidying up she did in the house. But the medical evidence told us that anyway." Mellish gave Matthew another of his long, intrusive stares. "I'm puzzled, however."

Matthew waited.

Mellish went on, "You seem to have the feeling that this man Staveley could be connected with your wife's death, but you haven't suggested the ghost of a motive. Did he kill her for having fallen in love with him when he hadn't with her? Did he find it so intolerable being loved by her that he had to strangle her?"

"No, of course not."

"Why, then?"

Matthew stood up. "I've been trying to answer that question ever since I found her dead. And all I've arrived at is either that I'm completely wrong and he doesn't come into the picture at all, or that she'd some kind of hold over him, knew something about him that was a serious danger to him."

"You mean she was blackmailing him?"

"Not in the ordinary sense, no. She'd never have been doing it for money. But she might have been trying to exert some sort of pressure on him, perhaps to make him leave his wife."

"What's sometimes called emotional blackmail."

"Yes, that's what I mean."

Mellish put his hands squarely on the desk and leant forward on them.

"You're sure you aren't trying to involve him simply because you've taken a dislike to him? You think your wife had fallen for him and you want him to pay for it."

"I'm not sure, no," Matthew answered. "I'm past trusting my own judgement."

"I see, I see. Well, it's an interesting theory. I must think about it. Meanwhile we'll go on watching for some more of your wife's jewellery to turn up." It was obvious that Mellish was not at all impressed. "You're going? Are you staying in London or returning to Fernley?"

"Returning to Fernley. I'm only up for the day."

They parted in a laboured exchange of politeness.

After that Matthew went to the genetics department at

Welford. Miss Graves greeted him with little cries of welcome. Letters had been piling up for him that obviously
should have been answered at once, only she had not
wanted to trouble him at Fernley, when she realised how
badly he must need undisturbed peace. But he could deal
with all those troublesome letters now, she said with a
happy little smile.

He dealt with most of them, as he usually did, by dump-
ing them in the waste paper basket. Miss Graves deplored
this and rescued a number so that she could compel him to
attend to them on another occasion, and one letter she
handed back to him, asking him with some sternness if he
was sure that it did not merit a reply.

Matthew re-read the letter. It was an invitation from the
Institute of Epigenetics in Melbourne, Australia, to spend a
year there. He was offered his travelling expenses and a generous salary. The invitation came from the Director of the
Institute, who not long ago had spent a year at Welford as a
post-doctoral fellow. He and Matthew had liked one another and done some interesting work together. In normal
circumstances Matthew would have found the invitation attractive.

At the moment he had no particular feelings about it, but
he put the letter aside. He left the department in time to get
himself a late lunch in a nearby pub. Afterwards he took a
taxi to the house agent where he had left his name to see if
they had any new flats on their books. They gave him one
or two addresses, but when he had looked at one flat he
dropped the idea of inspecting the others. It was nothing to
do with the flats themselves. One of them might be just what
would suit him. But in the mood that he was in, nothing
would appeal to him. His total lack of decision about his future made it impossible for him to form any other decisions.
About half past three he took another train back to Fernley.

When he arrived at the cottage he found Colin as usual at the table, writing industriously, and Cornelia busy with her knitting. She went on with it, her lips silently moving as she counted the stitches of her pattern, until she came to the end of a row, then looked up at Matthew.

"Well," she said, "how did it go?"

"I saw Mellish," Matthew said, sitting down opposite to her. "They've found a bracelet of Kate's."

"Found it—what do you mean?" she asked. "Somewhere in the house, was it?"

"No, a pawnbroker in Fulham turned it in to them. A small, dark girl with a North Country accent, who gave the name of Bradshaw, took it in to him."

"So it looks as if the idea about the burglar was right."

"It looks like it."

She let her knitting drop into her lap. "You don't sound satisfied."

He sighed. "What does it matter? They aren't going to find him."

"Why are you so sure?"

"Because . . . Oh, hell! Because I've certain feelings about the case, but one's feelings aren't evidence."

"But if a girl like that brought in the bracelet, there must have been a burglary, mustn't there?"

"I suppose so."

She frowned at him. "I wish there were some way of getting your mind off the problem. Whether they ever find the man or not, your life's got to go on and the sooner you accept that, the better."

"Well, I got an invitation to go to Australia for a year," Matthew said. "Shall I go?"

Colin swivelled round in his chair.

"Australia? Whereabouts?"

"Melbourne. The Institute of Epigenetics. Didn't you

meet Peter Wardle when he was over here a couple of years ago? He's Director of the Institute now and they're offering to pay all my travelling expenses and a salary."

"Yes, I remember him," Colin said. "Nice chap. But what about Welford? Will they let you go?"

"I should think so. I've taken no sabbatical leave since I went there, so I'm more than entitled to a year off."

"Will they go on paying your salary while you're away?" Cornelia asked.

"Oh yes, that's normal."

"Not that that matters to you now," she said. "I keep forgetting that. Of course you must go. It's the perfect answer to your problem."

"I'm not sure if the police would let me," Matthew said.

"When would you have to leave?"

"In the autumn, I suppose, at the beginning of the new academic year."

"Well, for the Lord's sake, the police aren't going to keep you hanging around all that time, are they? Of course they'll let you go." She gave him an inquiring glance. "Don't you *want* to go? Have you a sort of feeling you've got to stay hanging around here until something's discovered?"

"Perhaps I have."

"I'm sure that's wrong," she said, rolling up her knitting. "If I were you, I wouldn't hesitate. It'd do you a world of good. New scenes, new faces, and no one knowing too much about what's happened here. You could really get away from your ghosts. Do think about it, Matthew."

He stood up and stretched. "All right, I'll do that. Now I think I'll go for a short walk. I feel all nerves. It was talking to Mellish, I suppose, and getting nowhere. I shan't be long."

"I think it's going to rain," Colin said. "It's got that feeling."

"It doesn't matter." Matthew fetched his anorak from where it hung on a peg in the kitchen, took his walking-stick and set out into the twilight.

He walked further than he had intended, standing still every little while and gazing out at the dark chasm of the sea. To begin with, he felt a deep resistance to the idea of going abroad. Sheer inertia made him want to stay at home among familiar faces and following a familiar routine. He was old enough to have begun to feel that routine was very important to him. Only he had no home, that had to be remembered.

Striding along, feeling the first raindrops on his face and pulling up the hood of his anorak, he began to think more seriously than he had at first about the advantages of going to Melbourne. He liked travel. And if, as would be reasonable, the people at the Institute were ready to pay only for the shortest flight from London to Melbourne, he could add to the amount himself and go round the world while he was about it. He could go to Mexico, a thought that had always attracted him, and to Fiji and New Zealand. And on the way home he could spend some time in India. If he put out feelers he could probably get himself invited to do some lecturing there and pick up a few fees. And in Australia itself he would probably find time to do some exploring, see something of the desert, go to Alice Springs, see the Barrier Reef.

Apart from all of which, working again with Peter Wardle would be interesting. He had a lot of talent and was stimulating and he was always so full of his own concerns that he had very little time to take any great interest in yours. He would ask a few formal questions about Kate and that would be the end of that. With luck he might even be persuaded to keep the story of her death to himself. No one else in the Institute had known her and it was unlikely that an account of her not very dramatic murder had ever made the Melbourne papers.

Then when, in a year's time, Matthew returned to Welford, it would all be ancient history. The police might have caught her murderer or they might not, but Welford would have found plenty of other things to talk about. She could be quietly buried in the memories of a few people and normal life, of the kind that felt utterly impossible at the moment, could go on.

The rain was falling more heavily now and it had grown very dark. If Matthew had not known the path so well he might have strayed from it. When he turned back towards the cottage he saw the dim outlines of the Staveleys' house on his right, with lights on in one or two windows and with the two ghostly streaks in the garden of the borders filled with white daffodils. He was annoyed with himself now for having talked about them to Mellish, who had certainly taken Matthew for a fool. And no doubt he had been a fool to think about them at all. He passed the Welshes' small house, went on and let himself into the Naylors' cottage.

He knew at once that something was wrong. Cornelia was standing in front of the fireplace. She had a hand to her throat. Her eyes were staring. Slight, pale and defenceless-looking, she looked as if she would have liked to start screaming. Colin was sitting at the table, his face hidden in his hands, his fingers buried in his dark, curly hair. Matthew's first thought was that they had been quarrelling. He had never known them to quarrel and had no idea how they went about it. Most married couples, he believed, had their characteristic ways of quarrelling, from wild yelling to deadly silence, and their characteristic ways of making peace, but he had never known Colin and Cornelia to go any further than a little mild sarcasm at one another's expense.

He put his stick down and unzipped his anorak.

"You were right about the rain," he said. "It's turned into a rotten night."

Cornelia gave a kind of sob. He looked at her in surprise.

Colin raised his head. "There's been another one," he said. "A telephone call. I took it this time. I agree with you, I think it was a man's voice."

"What did he say?" Matthew asked, mopping his wet face with his handkerchief.

"As nearly as I can remember," Colin said, "he said, 'I loved her and I'm going to see you pay for it. You'll soon see how.' That was all. He rang off before I could say anything. I don't suppose he even realised he wasn't speaking to you."

"Well, I don't see why we should worry overmuch about it." Matthew felt surprisingly breezy. "Mellish told me he'd checked our alibis at the Volunteer. The barman remembers us. So this maniac can't do us any harm. Now what about a drink all round? For once you both look as if you need one even more than I do."

"The thing is, I'm fairly sure who's doing it," Cornelia said, brushing a hand across her eyes. "His saying he loved her, that really tells one everything."

"You mean Staveley," Matthew said.

"No, no, no!" she cried. "You've got him on the brain. I mean Ambrose. He was crazy about Kate. And talking about what he means to do! He's more than half-crazy, you must have seen that. He might do anything."

"This is the first time you've said anything about his being crazy about Kate," Matthew said, feeling wearily resentful, as if he had had some poor trick played upon him.

"Well, I could have been wrong," she said, "and in case I was, I didn't want to put you against him."

"You're only guessing now," Colin muttered.

"Shall I leave?" Matthew asked. "If I do you won't be bothered by any more of these calls."

"Of course not," Colin said. "Cornelia's dramatizing things. Even if it's Ambrose, he won't do anything."

She was rolling up her knitting. "How d'you know? I think he might. I think he might do anything."

"He'd have done something already, if he was going to," Colin said. "He goes in for talk a lot more than action. He just wants to upset us. You'll play into his hands if you worry too much about it."

"If you're so sure who it is," Matthew said, "shall I go and talk to him tomorrow? I'll do that, if you like—tell him about my talk with Mellish and that threatening me isn't going to get him anywhere."

Cornelia looked at him thoughtfully. "You mean talk to him quite openly? Accuse him of having made these calls?"

"Why not?"

She thrust her knitting into the workbag that hung from an arm of her chair.

"It might be the best thing to do," she said. "But let's think about it, shall we? I may have lost my head. You think yourself it's best to take no notice of the calls, don't you?"

"That's my own inclination," Matthew answered. "Talking of his being crazy about Kate, what were her feelings about him?"

"Non-existent, I'd say. And he isn't a person to take that too well. However . . ." She gave a shrug of her shoulders. "Now I'll get us something to eat. It's only going to be cold chicken and salad. I'm sorry I'm feeding you so badly, Matthew, but this situation's got under my skin in a way I can't explain. I feel quite disorganised. I'll try to do better tomorrow."

"Don't you think it would be best if I went back to London?" he suggested again.

"I'd guess that's what he wants," Colin said. "I'm sure the right thing to do is to ignore him. What about Australia, Matthew? Have you been thinking about it?"

"Yes, I think I'll go," Matthew said. "It'd solve a lot of problems."

Colin nodded. Cornelia went out to the kitchen. Matthew sat down in a chair by the fire.

"It's an odd thing," he said, "but I've got a feeling Cornelia's actually frightened."

"She'll get over it."

"But it isn't like her."

"As a matter of fact, I think she's more angry than frightened," Colin said. "At having been so wrong about Ambrose, you know. But perhaps by tomorrow she'll have decided the voice wasn't his, so the main thing is to give her time to calm down."

"Yes, I rather think that was my technique with her when we were young," Matthew said, "though it didn't always work. Did you think the voice might be Welsh's?"

"Could have been." Colin sounded as if he were becoming bored by the subject. He poured out drinks and disappeared with one of them after Cornelia into the kitchen.

They ate almost silently and soon afterwards Matthew went to bed to read for a while before trying to sleep. In the room below him the silence continued. Colin, he thought, was probably busy with his writing again and Cornelia with her knitting. He heard one of them presently turn on the television news and heard the voice of the announcer fill the room downstairs. Then one of them turned it off, crossed the room and began to rake at the embers in the grate to put the fire out before they went to bed. A few minutes later he heard them go upstairs to their room.

The rain beat on the windowpanes and a wind sighed in the chimney. He fell asleep with his book on his chest and the light on, to wake startled with a feeling of nightmare after what seemed a long time, to discover that it was only just after midnight and that he had probably been asleep for only a few minutes. Putting the book aside, he turned out the light, but then could not sleep. Presently he got up, went downstairs and made himself a cup of tea and while he was drinking it in the living room was filled with an almost uncontrollable desire to snatch up the telephone, dial Ambrose Welsh's number and when he answered simply breathe deeply at him—wasn't that said to be very frightening?—or perhaps laugh insanely. But he managed to check the impulse, reflecting that it might be just some such lunatic action that would herald the beginnings of insanity in himself. He finished his tea, went back to bed and this time slept soundly.

He was woken by commotion. Footsteps were coming and going, doors were slamming. Colin and Cornelia were talking at the same time and a third voice that Matthew did not recognise, though he felt that there was something familiar about it, now and then said something. He got up, only half-awake, pulled on some clothes and made for the stairs.

In a chair by the fireplace, which was littered with yesterday's dead ashes, Rachel Staveley was sitting bolt upright and shaking all over. Her face was dead white and her eyes were staring and wild. She was in an old raincoat, with her short hair damply plastered to her head. Cornelia, in a dressing gown, was standing beside her, holding a glass of brandy which she was trying to induce the other woman to drink, but she only recoiled from it and went on shuddering. The door to the garden stood wide open and rain was spattering the floor inside. There was no sign of Colin.

"It's Grant," Cornelia said. "He's fallen over the edge of the cliff and you can see him down on the rocks below. Eleanor and Tim are trying to climb down to see if they can help him and Rachel came here to get Colin. He knows the cliffs so well. And I've telephoned for Dr. Parkes and he's on his way over now."

"And the police?" Matthew asked. "Have you called them?"

Cornelia looked blank. "We didn't think of it. Ought we to do that?"

"At once. They're the people who can help most."

He reached for the telephone and dialled.

CHAPTER SIX

Matthew did not wait for the police to arrive. He pulled his anorak on and set off up the cliff path, leaving the two women together. The path was slippery from the rain that had gone on all night. Mud squelched under his shoes, though it was raining only lightly now and a narrow ray of sunshine was to be seen, coming through a rift in the cloud and making the drifting raindrops glisten.

He tramped up the path as far as the bench, from time to time stepping over the dilapidated wire fence to look down and see if there was anything below but rocks and surf. The tide was high. The rocks were almost covered, but except for the gulls perched on them there was only the leaping foam and the green, sliding, greedy water between them.

But when he reached the bench and again looked over the edge of the cliff into the depths, he saw the spread-eagled body on the rocks below, only just above the tide-mark. As he stood there, looking down, he saw Tim Welsh, followed after a moment by Eleanor Landon, start picking their way from the foot of the cliff that they had just descended towards the body. For a moment Matthew thought that Colin had not come here, then he saw him, almost hidden by an overhang of the cliff, clinging to it like a fly to a wall, about twenty feet down.

Seeing Matthew looking over, Colin shouted something at him, but the words were lost in the beating of the waves and the crying of the wind. Matthew made a gesture to show that he had not heard and Colin raised his voice and shouted again.

"Don't try to come down. I've been up and down here a dozen times, but you'll never make it. And you can't do anything."

That was Matthew's own feeling. He had no experience of rock-climbing, and if he tried to make his way down that wet, slippery cliff face, he thought that Colin would end up with two bodies on his hands, instead of one.

Cupping his hands about his mouth, Matthew shouted, "Are you sure he's dead?"

"Of course he is. Can't you see that?" Colin shouted back.

"I've called the police," Matthew yelled. "They'll be able to get him up."

"Good. Now I'd go back to help Cornelia with Rachel."

Colin resumed his progress downwards, reaching with assurance for handholds and footholds that Matthew could not have seen were there. But he did not return to the cottage. He remained where he was as Tim and Eleanor scrambled to the body on the rocks, bent over it, touched it, recoiled, then after a moment forced themselves to touch the stiff limbs again. Then he saw them stand up with a look of hopelessness and speak to one another inaudible words, lost in the wind and the rain. It was not long before Colin joined them. The three of them stood round the dead man, talking to one another at first, then falling silent.

Grant Staveley was wearing his green anorak with the hood back on his shoulders, showing his longish sandy hair plastered like seaweed across the thinning patch on his head. His heavy body looked flattened into an impossible, inhuman shape, with one leg thrust out at an angle that screamed of the enduring of intolerable pain. Yet perhaps there had really been very little pain, or even none at all.

Going over the edge of the cliff he might have lost consciousness immediately, or even if awareness had lasted
somehow until he struck the rocks below, surely it had been
blotted out instantly then.

Footsteps behind Matthew made him turn, then move
back from the edge of the cliff to the path. Dr. Parkes was
climbing up it. He greeted Matthew with a brief nod, then
went to the edge and looked down. Colin saw him and
waved with both arms.

"What does he mean?" Parkes asked.

"I think he's telling you not to try going down," Matthew
answered. "Unless you're a rock-climber, you'd find it dangerous."

"I shouldn't dream of going down," Parkes said. "I can't
stand heights and I value my life. And I've just looked in at
the Naylors' cottage and Mrs. Naylor told me you've sent
for the police. They'll bring tackle to bring him up. It isn't
as if there's anything I can do for him. D'you know, this
cliff is sometimes called Suicides' Cliff? Two or three people
go over it every year. Usually in fairly quick succession
too, which is interesting, as if one of them puts the idea into
the heads of the others."

"Then has someone been over here recently?" Matthew
asked.

"Not since last summer. It's usually tourists who do it,
not natives."

"But you think it's suicide?"

"Oh, my dear chap, I haven't the least idea." The doctor
shrugged his shoulders. "But accident seems unlikely.
Staveley's been living here for some time. He knows this
path too well to wander off it."

"Last night was a very dark night, once it started to
rain," Matthew said.

"Well, it could have been accident, then, I suppose, or a

coronary—something like that. There'll have to be a post mortem. We may know more after it. Staveley never struck me as a suicidal type, as a matter of fact, but you never know, especially with these artistic characters. I remember being at a party once and getting talking to a man who told me he was a poet. We had a long, interesting talk. I liked him. I hadn't realised a poet could be such a normal, human sort of chap. Interested in football, told me he was hoping to get married soon. We arranged to meet again. And that night he swallowed a whole bottle of aspirins and was found dead in the morning. I've never forgotten it."

"Hallo there," said the voice of Ambrose Welsh, who had just pushed open the gate in his garden wall and was climbing up the path towards them. "Tim and the girl got down all right, did they? Good, good. I used to try to cure Tim of climbing around here, you know, but I never got anywhere. He's quiet, but he's stubborn. And lately he's taken Eleanor up and down a number of times. I think she got quite a kick out of it. But when Staveley found out about it he came round to us and made a hell of a scene. I thought he was going to take Tim by the throat. But Tim was a lot the bigger of the two and even Staveley had the sense to realise it. I'm told the police are coming."

Welsh's voice was not exactly cheerful, but certainly there was very little concern in it.

"You've been out here already, then?" Matthew said.

"Yes, when Rachel and Eleanor saw Staveley down there, Eleanor ran straight in to us to get Tim," Welsh answered, "and I came out with them to see what had happened. When I saw it I advised Rachel to go straight down to get Colin to come up here. He's the most useful person around here in a crisis of this sort. I see he's down there now. Too late to do any good, of course. I suppose Staveley's been dead for hours, hasn't he, Parkes?"

"You can hardly believe I can tell you that from this distance," Parkes replied.

"What did you do yourself when you'd told the others what to do?" Matthew asked Welsh.

"Went back into the house to finish my breakfast," Welsh answered. "It wasn't going to help anyone if I just stood around. We elderly ones may as well accept our limitations. Then I thought of telephoning the police and was told someone had already done that—" He stopped abruptly. "Hallo, hallo," he said, "how did this get here?"

Welsh walked quickly to the bench. Matthew and Parkes turned to see what had caught his attention. Lying on the bench was a walking-stick which Matthew for a moment took for his own. It was a malacca cane with a silver collar at the top of it, engraved with initials, and a deer-horn handle. But Matthew remembered clearly that he had taken his stick back to the cottage with him the evening before and had put it into the umbrella stand there. He also remembered that Staveley possessed a stick that looked exactly like it.

Welsh was reaching out to pick up the stick when Matthew thrust his hand aside and said, "I shouldn't do that."

"Why the hell not?" Welsh asked irritably. "What d'you think I'm going to do with it, pitch it over the cliff? . . . Oh, I see." The furrows in his high forehead smoothed out. "You think it's evidence. Best not to touch it in case it's got something to tell us. Quite right. I should have thought of that myself. It does belong to Staveley, I suppose."

"It did."

"Yes, did—exactly. Evidence of what, though? D'you think someone snatched it from him and bashed him over the head with it and pushed him over the cliff? Doesn't seem likely to me. Anyone who did that would have thrown the stick after him, wouldn't they? They wouldn't have put it down carefully on the bench to be found. I don't think much of your theory."

"It isn't my theory," Matthew said. "If it's anyone's, it's your own."

Welsh frowned again. "You're a prickly character, do you know that? You jump on one, whatever one says to you. I understand you've been under a strain recently, of course, and the present situation is very upsetting, but I don't see why you should take it out on me."

"I'm sorry," Matthew said. "I didn't mean to."

But he had meant to, he realised, simply because Welsh did not show any signs of finding the present situation in the least upsetting. Rather, he seemed to find it exhilarating. Matthew was glad to hear voices before he himself was tempted to say any more and to see several uniformed men advancing up the path.

They had brought ropes with them and other tackle. They all knew the doctor and stood chatting to him for a moment before they began to organize the rescue party. The man in charge, a sergeant, indicated to Matthew and Welsh that they could not be of any assistance. In other words, he wanted them out of the way.

Welsh looked at Matthew and said, "Like to come in with me for some coffee?"

"Thanks, but I think I'd better get back to Cornelia," Matthew answered, "to see how she's managing with Mrs. Staveley." He turned to the sergeant. "We found this stick on the bench when we got here. It belongs to Mr. Staveley, I believe. We haven't moved it. It was just like that when we found it."

"I see, sir, thank you." The sergeant was more interested in helping to fasten a rope round the body of one of his men than he was in the stick. "All right now, Jim, take it easy."

They moved to the edge of the cliff. Ambrose Welsh turned in at his garden gate and Matthew went down the muddy path to the Naylors' cottage.

There was silence in the living room when he walked into it. Rachel Staveley was still sitting in the chair where he had left her, but she had stopped shaking and was sitting back limply against the cushions. Her face was ashen, with big round holes for eyes. The brandy that Cornelia had tried to make her drink was still in its glass on the mantelpiece, but she was sipping from a mug of black coffee.

"Like some coffee, Matthew?" Cornelia asked. She had got dressed in her jeans and sweater since Matthew had left the cottage. "I've only just made it."

"Thank you, I should," Matthew said and took the mug that she poured out for him. "I'm sorry to bring you bad news, Mrs. Staveley, but there doesn't seem to be any hope. Colin's down there now with the other two and he signalled to us that there's nothing to be done."

"Of course there isn't," she answered in her soft, expressionless voice. "Are the others safe?"

"Yes, and the police are going down to them now."

"Those cliffs are so dangerous," she said. "Grant always said so. It was one of the things he had against Tim that he took Eleanor climbing on them without Grant's knowing anything about it. Of course, he stopped it as soon as he found out. It was a pity, in a way, because Tim's a nice boy and I was so pleased when I thought he and Eleanor were falling in love. Living here, you see, she doesn't see as many young people as she ought to, so I was delighted when she met Tim. But Grant always said he wasn't nearly good enough for her and anyway they were too young and if they married it'd only make a mess of both their lives. It was what we quarrelled about yesterday evening and why Grant went out into the dark. I think it may even have been why he decided to do what he did."

Cornelia gave her a swift look, then caught Matthew's eye and slightly shook her head. He spoke all the same.

"What he did?" he said. "Do you mean you believe he went over that cliff on purpose?"

"But of course," she said in a tone of weary patience. "It couldn't have been an accident. He knew every inch of that path. Besides, he was wonderfully sure-footed. But he often said he didn't know why he went on living, he'd never be a great painter and that was all that mattered. Then he'd get very drunk sometimes and talk of killing himself. I never thought he meant it, but he must have, mustn't he? He'd been doing a lot of drinking lately because some painting was going badly and I was very stupid to let him quarrel with me, about Eleanor, of all things. He'd get really angry if I argued with him about her. He even struck me once. Then he was so full of shame afterwards I was quite scared about what he might do."

"Did he strike you yesterday?" Matthew asked.

"Oh no, he just cursed me and Eleanor and everyone else and dashed out of the house. I told him it was going to rain, but he took no notice. And he didn't come home for supper, so I supposed he'd gone down to the pub, as he sometimes did, and presently I went to bed and went to sleep and it was only when I woke up in the morning that I discovered he'd never come in at all. So Eleanor and I went out looking for him and we saw him down there on the rocks. We don't know when he went over."

She was talking now in her gentle voice as if she could not stop.

As if she heard this herself, she suddenly forced her lips shut and closed her eyes, trying to withdraw into some secret place where nothing was to be heard or seen and no

one could reach her. But it was only for a moment. Opening
her eyes again, she held out her mug.

"Can I have some more coffee, Cornelia?"

Cornelia took the mug and refilled it.

"Could you manage some breakfast now?" she suggested.
"You've had nothing to eat since you got up this morning."

"Oh no, thank you, I couldn't eat anything," Rachel said,
"but the coffee really helps."

"Matthew, what about you?"

It surprised him to realise that he was extremely hungry,
but with the white-faced woman sitting there, trying to take
in the fact that her husband was dead, it did not seem the
time to ask for bacon and eggs.

"Later, perhaps," he said. "I'll get the fire going, shall I?"

Cornelia looked startled. "How stupid of me! I should
have thought of that. Yes, will you, please?"

He went out into the kitchen and through the back door
to the lean-to where the Naylors kept their firewood and,
collecting a few logs and some kindling, returned to the living room, knelt in front of the fireplace, raked the ashes
aside and set the fire going. The kindling crackled and spat,
and as if it had taken this to make Rachel realise how cold
she was, she gave a convulsive shiver. But after the one
tremor, she sat quite still.

"That's nice," she said absently as flames leapt up the
chimney. "'Apple wood green, fit for a queen . . .' That's
what we used to say when we were children and lived right
out in the country. We'd no electricity, no main drainage,
or anything, but it was beautiful. We were great friends
then, Grant and I. He used to paint even then, you know,
and I used to hero-worship him, I thought he was so clever.
And he was, of course. I sometimes think he was far
more talented than he himself ever realised. Whatever he
achieved, he always demanded more of himself. He was

never satisfied. That's why he was so dissatisfied with me and everything."

Cornelia was looking bewildered. "It isn't apple wood," she said. "At least, I don't think it is. I think it's sycamore or something like that. We get it from an old gypsy who comes round with a cart."

Rachel, looking musingly at the leaping flames, did not seem to hear her.

Matthew said gently, "Then you and your husband knew each other for a long time before you married, did you?"

"Well, yes and no," she answered. "As children we loved one another. My father was the vicar and his father was our gardener and we used to play together every day. And it was my father who realised how gifted Grant was and helped him with his education and got him sent to an art school. But long before that I'd been sent to a boarding school and somehow that separated us. I suppose it was just adolescence, but we got self-conscious with one another and when we met we had hardly anything to say. And then, much later, long after my first husband was killed and I'd been living here for some years, Grant came here by chance, and . . ." She paused and abruptly repeated the closing of her lips and eyes, willing herself to be silent.

When she opened her eyes again, she gave a long sigh, leaning forward, gazing into the fire as if she were aware of nothing else in the room.

"Mrs. Staveley, are you sure your husband was drunk when he went out yesterday evening?" Matthew asked.

She did not look at him. "Well, moderately so. Why?"

"I was only thinking that if he was drunk he might easily have gone over the edge of the cliff accidentally, however well he knew the path," he said. "And it really was very dark last night."

"Yes, I know. When he'd gone and I was beginning to

have the feeling that the quarrel was all my fault, I went to
the door and looked out, wanting to call him back or perhaps follow him. Then it was so black outside, I went back
indoors. And if I hadn't, if I'd followed my first impulse and
gone after him, he'd be alive now, wouldn't he? Will I ever
get rid of that thought, I wonder."

She gave another of her deep, painful sighs.

The strange thing about it to Matthew was that he could
hear no grief in it. Pity for the dead man, yes, and remorse
because of how she had failed him, but not any sense of intolerable loss. He was puzzled because it reminded him of
something. Then suddenly he saw a picture of himself sitting in the silent room in the Golders Green house, with
Kate's body on the hearthrug before him, while he tried to
will himself to go to the telephone to call the police. As he
had been then, he thought, what she was mourning now was
not a death, but the final ending of a dream that had not
had much existence for a long time.

"You mustn't blame yourself," Cornelia said with a touch
of impatience in her voice. With nothing practical to do she
was soon at a loss. "Now I'm going to get some breakfast
and you're going to eat it, even if it's just some cornflakes.
You don't know what's ahead of you today. For one thing,
the police will want to talk to you. It may be pretty awful.
But you'll feel better if you've some food inside you."

She went out to the kitchen.

When she had gone Rachel looked round at Matthew
with a small twitch of a smile. On her strained face it
looked almost grotesque.

"I wish I were one of those people who always know
what to do," she said. "I've never known. I've made a mess
of my life and several other people's."

He smiled back at her. "Do you want those cornflakes?"

"No."

"Then perhaps Cornelia isn't really right to make you eat them."

"Oh, I'm sure I'll feel better if I do—if I'm not sick. Matthew, when Kate died . . ." She hesitated.

"Yes?"

"You blamed yourself, didn't you, even though you'd nothing to blame yourself for? Didn't you blame yourself for being alive when she was dead?"

"Yes, but in my case it happens there's someone who blames me for a lot more than that. I'm talking about my friend on the telephone."

"Who you thought was Grant, didn't you?"

He turned away from her so that she could not see his face. "What made you think that?"

"The way you looked at him the other night at the party here. You looked at him with hatred. He spoke about it on the way home and laughed about it."

He turned back to her. "Well, was I right?"

"I wish I knew," she said softly.

It silenced Matthew as completely as anything that she could have said.

Presently Cornelia came in with fresh coffee, cornflakes and scrambled eggs on toast. Rachel made an effort to eat a certain amount, more out of courtesy to Cornelia, Matthew thought, than because she had the least desire for food. He himself ate hungrily, but when Colin came in a short time later and asked at once for breakfast, there was more than enough left over for him. His clothes were torn and mud-stained and his hands were scored with deep scratches. He ate standing up and although he spoke to Rachel, he avoided looking directly at her, as if a personal contact with her were more than he could face.

"They've brought him up on a stretcher," he said, "and they're taking him to the mortuary. They say he's been dead

for hours. And then, of course, they're going to want to talk
to you. I think they'll make it as easy for you as possible.
The man in charge now is an Inspector Drayton, who seems
a reasonable sort of chap. I don't know if you'd sooner see
him here or go home. If that's what you want to do, Cornelia and I will go with you, of course."

"Where's Eleanor?" she asked anxiously.

Colin gave a glance over his shoulder, as if he had only
just realised that Eleanor and Tim had not come into the
room with him.

"They'll be along," he said. "They were talking to Drayton when I left."

"They're all right, are they, they're quite safe?"

"Oh yes."

"Those cliffs are so horrible. You've hurt yourself, Colin,
going down."

He glanced at his hands, where blood had congealed
along the scratches.

"It's nothing," he said. "The rock's rough in places. How
are you, Rachel? D'you want to see Parkes again? He's still
out there. If you'd like a sedative or something—"

"No!" she interrupted him in a high voice. "I don't want
anything. Not now. I'll talk to the police and tell them all
about the quarrel I had with Grant yesterday and how he
went out and didn't come back and why I think it's suicide.
I'll tell them everything I can, then perhaps I'll ask for a
sedative, or just drink up that brandy of yours. I might even
get drunk. I'll have to get through the day somehow, shan't
I? I don't suppose it matters much how I do it."

"Suicide?" Colin said. "But surely—"

He broke off as the door opened again and Eleanor and
Tim came in.

Eleanor went straight to her mother, who stood up at
once and put her arms round her daughter. Eleanor hid her

face on her mother's shoulder and began to cry uncontrollably. To Matthew it seemed somehow curious that in the circumstances it should be the mother who was consoling the daughter and not the daughter the mother. He remembered, when his own father had died, what a tremendous burden of responsibility he had immediately felt for comforting his mother. But his parents' marriage had been a good one. He supposed that what he was seeing now meant merely that Eleanor had been far more deeply attached to her stepfather than Rachel to her husband, and that Rachel accepted it now as normal that it was the girl who needed support.

He looked at Colin. "Are the police sure it was an accident?"

Tim answered, "Well, it's a bit odd really. There's a walking-stick of Mr. Staveley's on the bench up there, and they seem to think that if he'd gone over the cliff accidentally, it would have fallen with him. Or he might have dropped it somewhere in the grass. But he wouldn't have laid it down carefully on the bench. I suppose that makes sense. But I don't know how seriously they're taking it. One of the men suggested it and Inspector Drayton seemed interested."

Cornelia was pouring out coffee for Tim, whose hands, like Colin's, were rubbed raw by the rock of the cliffs.

"They're talking about something else as well," Tim went on, taking the hot coffee gratefully. "They're talking about whether Mr. Staveley could have been pushed."

Rachel let go of Eleanor abruptly. "No!" she exclaimed. "I don't believe it."

"Well, there's something about the stick that worries them," Tim said. "They didn't mean Eleanor and me to hear, but they were talking about fingerprints and saying something about how there wouldn't be any after it had been out all night in the rain, and one of them said there wouldn't be any on a horn handle anyway, all of which adds up, it seems to me, to saying they think someone could have grabbed the stick and used it to drive Mr. Staveley off the cliff."

"If I'd committed a murder like that," Matthew said, "I wouldn't have laid the stick down tidily on the bench, I'd have thrown it over the edge of the cliff after Staveley."

Rachel looked at him over her daughter's shoulder with a sudden spark in her hollow eyes. But her voice was as level as usual as she remarked, "It sounds as if you're quite a specialist in murder, Matthew. Now, Cornelia, I think I'll be going home. It'll be most convenient for everyone if the police talk to me there. Eleanor can come with me, and Tim too, if he likes, so there's no need for you and Colin to come, though it was very thoughtful of Colin to suggest it. And I can't thank you enough for your kindness to me this morning." She crossed the room to Cornelia and kissed her cheek, then put an arm through Eleanor's and said, "Come, we're going home."

Eleanor mopped her eyes with her sleeve in the gesture of a child, gave Matthew a quick look that was not childish at all and let herself be led out of the room. Tim followed.

The police did not come to the cottage till the early afternoon. Two men came then, Inspector Drayton and a man whom he introduced as Sergeant Bolting. The sergeant carried a walking-stick which Matthew assumed was Grant Staveley's. Inspector Drayton said there were a few questions that he would like to ask Professor Tierney and that he could do it here, if that was convenient, or if the professor preferred it, he could come to the police station. The Inspector had an oddly apologetic manner, as if the cloak of authority did not fit him too well. He was a man of medium height, with a reserved face, evasive grey eyes, a pallid complexion and straw-coloured hair. He had an air of wanting, above all, to be inconspicuous. The sergeant was several inches taller than he was and heavily built, with protuberant eyes in a heavy, ruddy face and plump jowls bulging above his shirt-collar. He looked far the more assertive of the two men, yet as Matthew soon noticed, he left all the talking to the Inspector.

"Come in, of course," Cornelia said, holding the door open for the two men to enter. "Do you want to talk to my brother alone? We haven't much room here, but my husband and I can go upstairs to be out of your way."

"I don't think there's any need for that," Drayton answered. "Perhaps you and Mr. Naylor may be able to help us. Of course, it's Mr. Staveley's death that we're concerned with." He turned to Matthew. "May I ask, Professor Tierney, did you see Mr. Staveley yesterday?"

The two detectives had taken the chairs that Colin had offered them. Matthew remained standing with an elbow on the mantelpiece.

"No," he said, "I went to London yesterday."

"Yes, we know that," Drayton said. "You saw Mr. Mellish, didn't you? But after you came back, didn't you see Mr. Staveley?"

"No," Matthew repeated.

"When did you see him last?"

Cornelia broke in, "At a small party we gave here the day before yesterday. Mr. and Mrs. Staveley came to it with Miss Landon."

"I'd like Professor Tierney to answer for himself, if you don't mind," Drayton said. He raised pale eyebrows inquiringly at Matthew.

"My sister's quite right," Matthew said. "In fact, I only met Mr. Staveley twice. Once was at that party and once was on the day before it, when Mr. Naylor and I went out for a walk along the cliff path and happened to meet Mr. Staveley and his stepdaughter."

"Did you go for a walk yesterday along the cliff path after you got back from London?" Drayton asked.

Matthew nodded, wondering how the Inspector knew of it.

"Yes, I did."

"Although it was raining."

"It hadn't begun yet when I started out and it happened I'd a problem I wanted to think out. I often go walking when I want to think and I didn't realise how heavily it was going to rain later."

"But you didn't meet Mr. Staveley?"

"No. Why do you think I did?"

Drayton did not answer the question. "Did you meet any-body?"

"Not that I remember."

"You didn't sit on the bench up there and talk to any-one?"

"It was hardly weather for sitting chatting on benches."

"But if the rain hadn't started yet . . ."

Matthew did his best to meet the Inspector's evasive eyes, but succeeded only for an instant, when their shrewdness disconcerted him. Then they turned, as if there were safety there, to dwell on the big, red face of the sergeant.

"If someone's told you they saw me there," Matthew said, "it isn't true."

Drayton shook his head. "No one's said anything of the sort, but we found this stick on the bench and we believe it's yours."

"Oh, I see," Matthew said. "No, it isn't mine. It belonged to Mr. Staveley. I've one that's almost identical, but it's over there in that umbrella stand. I believe that kind of malacca cane with the silver collar on it, engraved with initials, and the deer-horn handle was a standard pattern for Edwardian gentlemen. Mine belonged to my father and Staveley said his belonged to his. That was on my first day here, when my brother-in-law and I met Staveley and his stepdaughter on the path, as I was telling you. We said something to one another about how alike the sticks were."

"But Mr. Staveley's father's initials wouldn't have been J.K.T., would they?" Drayton said. "They'd have been something ending in S." He reached out for the walking-stick that the sergeant was holding. "Would you look at this, Professor, and tell me if it isn't yours?"

He held the stick out to Matthew.

He took it and turned it to the light, so that the initials on the silver showed clearly.

"Yes," he said after a moment. "J.K.T. This is my stick. So the one I was carrying yesterday must be Staveley's. Just let me see. . . ." He crossed to the umbrella stand and plucked out the stick that looked exactly like the one that he was holding. "Yes, G.L.S.," he said. "But I don't know how the two got mixed up."

"Unless you met and talked on the bench yesterday evening and you took the wrong stick away with you." Drayton reached out to take the two sticks away from Matthew. He looked thoughtfully at the initials on each, then suddenly looked up at Matthew, letting their eyes at last meet directly. "I think I should tell you what Mr. Mellish said to me on the telephone this morning," he said. "He told me you appeared to be convinced that Mr. Staveley had murdered your wife. You advanced no evidence for it, but he was sure you believed it. And if you did, rightly or wrongly, it might, it seems to me, have given you a good reason for pushing Mr. Staveley off the cliff. And you might have left what you thought was his stick behind on the bench to make it look as if he had done this deliberately and had in fact committed suicide."

CHAPTER SEVEN

"But that's absurd!" Cornelia cried out angrily. "I can tell you exactly how the sticks got mixed up. It happened the evening of our party. Mr. Staveley was carrying his stick when he arrived here and he put it straight into the stand. And when he left he took the wrong stick away with him. That's all. It's perfectly simple."

"I see," Drayton said, but he went on looking at Matthew as he asked, "Are you quite sure of that, Mrs. Naylor?"

"Absolutely sure," she answered.

"Mr. Staveley was carrying his stick when he came here?"

"Yes."

"Yes, he was," Colin said. "I happened to notice it too."

"So Professor Tierney was carrying Mr. Staveley's stick when he went out yesterday evening."

"I must have been," Matthew said.

Drayton took a moment to think before he came out with his next question. "Didn't you notice anything about it, the grip or the weight, that felt different from the one you're used to?"

"I'm not so very used to it," Matthew said. "It belonged to my sister for years. She gave it to me only the other day."

"I see," Drayton said again. He stood up. The sergeant stood up beside him. "You'll be staying here for a little while, will you, Professor Tierney?"

"A little while, yes," Matthew said. "I haven't decided how long."

"We'll take both sticks with us, if you don't mind," Drayton went on. "I'll have to ask Mrs. Staveley to identify the one you say is her husband's and see if she confirms that he brought it with him to your house."

"Shall we get ours back?" Cornelia asked.

"No doubt," he said. "But we'll have to keep it for a little while. I'm sure you understand that."

"It's just that it belonged to our father and we value it," she said.

"We'll take good care of it." Drayton gave a bleak little smile.

To Matthew there was more of a threat in it than reassurance. Taking the two sticks with them, the detectives left the cottage.

As soon as they had gone, Cornelia exploded, "He didn't believe me! Asking Rachel if Grant really did bring that stick here with him!"

"Well, she'll say he did," Colin said, "so it doesn't matter."

"Suppose she doesn't! Suppose she's forgotten!"

"That's unlikely. Don't worry."

"I suppose he really did bring the stick with him to the party," Matthew said. "I didn't notice it myself."

Colin and Cornelia were both silent for a moment, looking at one another. Then Colin laughed.

"How much will you pay us for going on saying we did?" he asked.

Matthew hesitated, then laughed too. "Sorry," he said.

"After all, there's no other way the sticks could have got mixed up," Cornelia said.

"Really it's a pity you ever admitted you went for that walk yesterday evening," Colin said. "If you're right that no one saw you and you'd said you hadn't been out all the evening and Cornelia and I had backed you up, you'd have a perfect alibi for Grant's death."

"That would have been two alibis you'd given me, plus explaining how the sticks got mixed up," Matthew said. "The police might have found that rather much of a good thing."

"I suppose sticking to the truth has its virtues," Colin said.

"But the police aren't going to suspect Matthew of murdering Grant, are they?" Cornelia said, looking at Colin, then at Matthew, then back to Colin with so much anxiety on her face that Matthew was moved. After their stormy childhood it still took him by surprise when he saw that Cornelia, in maturity, had become fond of him.

"If they do, they'll have a pretty thin case," he said.

Colin sat down in the chair that Inspector Drayton had occupied, and put his elbows on the table and his head in his hands. The torn skin on them still showed as dark red weals, though the blood on them had been washed away.

"It's clear what we ought to do, of course," he said. "That's to look for the real murderer. If there was one. And if there wasn't, which is probable, we try to prove it. At the moment I haven't the slightest idea how we go about it, but I'm sure two scientific chaps like us ought to be able to mount an investigation. We have an advantage over the police, which is that we can start with the premise that Matthew is innocent. Now, what about some tea?"

Cornelia nodded and was turning away to the kitchen when there was a loud knock on the door.

Colin opened it. Ambrose Welsh stood outside. He glanced past Colin into the room before he spoke.

"Police gone, I see," he said. "I came along a little while ago, but I saw their car outside, so I thought I'd wait. I had a dose of them myself before lunch. Someone's been telling them I didn't get on with Staveley, so they seem to be wondering if I pushed him off the cliff. I told them there have been hundreds of people in my lifetime I didn't get on with, but I've never yet been driven to murder. That pale chap, the Inspector, looked as if he didn't believe a word I said."

Cornelia had stood aside to let him into the room and closed the door after him.

"We thought he'd chosen Matthew as chief suspect," she said.

"So that's his technique, is it?" Welsh said. "Scare the daylights out of everyone in turn and see if anyone starts to tremble, or looks him too straight in the eye, or does anything else unnatural. I hope he wasn't too rough on Rachel."

"He wasn't exactly rough on Matthew," Cornelia said. "He was just insinuating."

Matthew thought that Drayton had gone rather further than merely to insinuate suspicion. His own impression was that the Inspector had come pretty close to a direct accusation. Yet when he tried to remember just what the man had said, he felt oddly confused. But that, he thought, was his own fault. He had been in a state of confusion ever since Kate's death. Nothing was coherent. Nothing made sense. Suspicion, from his own suspicion, based on Kate's sudden liking for white flowers, that Grant Staveley had been her lover, to Drayton's suspicion that he had murdered Staveley, had an anaesthetic effect on the rational faculty. That he was not the only person under suspicion did not clear the air in the least. Looking at Welsh in a wondering way, he tried to see some resemblance between the man and himself, a resemblance which could make Drayton think them equally capable of murder.

Murderers, however, as was well known, came in all shapes and sizes. Welsh, with his birdlike thinness, his look of being made of wire springs, his narrow face and sharp, aggressive features, was totally unlike Matthew, with his tall, slightly stooping figure and round mild face. But those things would be merely superficial dissimilarities to Drayton.

"I was just going to make some tea," Cornelia said.

"Ah, that's just what I feel like," Welsh said. "I don't often bother with tea in the afternoon. I generally hold out till it's time for a drink. But I'm all at sixes and sevens today. Too many things happening. I don't like it. I don't seem able to settle down to anything. That's why I came along. What do you think really happened to Staveley?"

"I think it was an accident," Cornelia replied. "Rachel thinks it was suicide. The police seem to think it was murder. Take your pick."

She went out to the kitchen.

"And you, Colin?" Welsh asked. "What do you think it was?"

"I haven't made up my mind," Colin said. "But it seems to me the police could perhaps do with a little help, and the first thing for us to do is to think over if there's anyone we know of who had it in for Grant enough to kill him."

Welsh nodded gravely. "Yes, and I think I can help there. I've been turning that over in my own mind ever since the police came to see me. First of all, you see, I tried to see things from their point of view. I considered their case against me and I came to the conclusion they had one of a sort. That quarrel between Staveley and me about getting me out of my house and developing the land was really quite serious and I never for a moment believed he'd given up the scheme. I happen to know he'd been going to work on several members of the planning committee, and if he'd succeeded in forcing me out I'm not sure what I mightn't have done. I don't think I'd ever have gone quite as far as planning to murder him deliberately, but if we'd met out on the cliffs one evening, both of us having had one or two drinks too many, I think we might have started brawling and I might have pushed him over the edge."

"By mistake on purpose, so to speak," Colin suggested.

"Yes, you could put it that way."

"I agree it's possible," Colin said. "Have you any alibi for yesterday evening?"

"Not much of one. Tim and I spent it at home. Tim was working on a nice little Regency escritoire he's restoring and I was reading. But an alibi in the family isn't a very convincing thing, as you yourselves know only too well. However, I haven't been thinking only about my own case. I've found motives for a number of other people. Take Tim, for instance."

"In spite of his being at home?"

"There's no one but myself to say he was and I, naturally, would back him to the hilt, whatever the truth was. And Staveley really hated Tim, you know. It went very deep with him."

"Did Tim hate Grant?" Colin asked. "That's the relevant question, isn't it?"

"Tim never hated anybody in his life," Welsh said. "Even years of exposure to me haven't soured him. He's the most good-natured clown you ever met. He's very like his mother. She was a wonderfully good-natured woman. I've never known anyone like her."

"Then wouldn't it have been Grant who murdered Tim and not the other way about?"

"Tim doesn't know his own strength. And I didn't say he isn't capable of losing his temper. It can be quite explosive. But it's all over in a matter of minutes and he blames himself desperately for it afterwards and there's no hatred in it, just acute exasperation. But those few moments of exasperation could have happened up there on the cliff. Not that I think he'd ever have left Staveley lying down on the rocks all night. As soon as he saw what he'd done, he'd have gone climbing down straight away, even in the darkness, to see if there was anything he could do."

"Just what would the exasperation have been about?" Colin asked.

"That's more complicated than it seems. There's the obvious reason, that Staveley was trying to break up the love affair between Tim and Eleanor. Tim adores that girl. He's crazy about her. Whether she's quite as crazy about him . . . However, I'll come back to that presently. It's a fact, anyway, that for the first time in his young life Tim's been absolutely bowled over. And he believes that she has been too and can't see any reason why they shouldn't get married. They may seem rather young for marriage to people of our generation, but for his it's normal. Only Staveley wouldn't hear of it. Not that he could stop it legally, but he could have used all the influence he had on Eleanor, and there's no question he had a great deal, to prevent it. So there's your one reason."

"What you called the obvious reason," Colin said. "What's the other?"

Welsh shifted uneasily in his chair. "You're going to say I'm a nasty-minded old man, but the fact is, you know, there was something not quite normal about Staveley's love for Eleanor. Or if these things are actually more normal than one supposes, something not quite socially acceptable. Haven't you noticed it yourself?"

"Perhaps I have," Colin said. "Overpossessive fathers aren't unheard of. So you think Tim might have murdered Grant because he was outraged by the thought of an incestuous relationship between him and Eleanor."

"Not on your life!" Welsh exclaimed. "Tim's much too

innocent to think of a thing like that. But he might simply have felt that Eleanor was more subservient to Staveley than he could understand and have murdered out of simple jealousy."

"And Eleanor? You said you were coming back to her."

"Yes, poor child," Welsh said. "Caught between the devil and the deep. Very, very deep waters, that's what we're getting into when we start thinking about her. Let's begin at the shallow end. Like Tim, she might simply have been enraged with Staveley for coming between her and Tim. And remember that she's a muscular young woman who might have been able to push Staveley off the cliff if she took him by surprise. That's the simple explanation of what could have happened. But there's a quite different explanation and it's a very ugly one." He shot a sudden look at Matthew. "We haven't been talking about your wife, but I suppose this is where she comes into the story. Do you mind if I go on?"

"Go on," Matthew said.

"Well, she and Staveley saw a great deal of one another when she was here," Welsh continued. "He painted her portrait. And if the incestuous feeling wasn't only on Staveley's side, but on Eleanor's too, she might have been eaten up with jealousy. She's a passionate child, without any great supply of intelligence. She might have been quite unable to bear what she saw developing between Staveley and your wife and have been the person who went to London and killed her. As I was saying, she's young and strong. She could have done it. And Staveley might have realised it and been horrified at what she'd done and let the girl see it and in her bitterness she might have killed him."

Colin was looking at Welsh with a worried frown. "Do you believe a word you're saying, Ambrose?"

Welsh gave a cackle of laughter. "Believe it? Good Lord,

no, I'm just hypothesizing. I haven't even started on Rachel."

"So she comes next, does she?" Colin said. "Well, go on."

"Actually, she seems to me the person with far the strongest motive for killing Staveley," Welsh said. "That's generally true of the wife or the husband, as the case may be, isn't it? She could have been jealous of Mrs. Tierney. She could have been jealous of her own daughter. She could have been revolted at what she thought Staveley was doing to Eleanor. She could simply have built up over the years a hatred of her husband that became more than she could bear. She may just have disliked his painting as much as I did and thought it was time he was stopped. Oh, I think Rachel makes a splendid suspect."

Cornelia came in from the kitchen with the tea-tray.

"I don't think I like this conversation much," she said. "Sugar, Ambrose?"

"Yes, please, three spoonfuls," he said. "I'm sorry you don't like it, Cornelia. I was just getting into my stride, but I'll stop if you say so."

"No, go on," Colin said. "Who's coming next?"

"I was just going to start on Professor Tierney," Welsh said. "But he's probably had more than enough of this sort of thing. Let's change the subject."

"No," Matthew said. "I'd like to hear if you've anything new to add to it."

"I'm sure I haven't." Welsh stirred his tea vigorously. "The police are really very efficient and you're the one person they've had time to investigate. They'll certainly have thought of the possibility that you killed Staveley because you thought he'd murdered your wife."

Matthew nodded. "They have."

"It could also have been out of simple jealousy because she'd fallen in love with him."

"Yes," Matthew agreed.

"Are you a jealous man?"

"Not very."

"Then it could have been because you had reason to believe he was your anonymous caller whom Cornelia told us about the other evening and that you'd some reason to fear him, even if there wasn't a hole in your alibi."

"Have you any idea why I should fear him?" Matthew asked.

"Oh, ideas!" Welsh said. He drank some of his tea. "I always have so many of them, they keep me awake at night. It's a terrible thing being cursed with an imagination."

"I don't believe you've any idea at all about our anonymous caller," Cornelia said. "You're just bluffing."

"All right, my dear, that's what I'm doing, bluffing. This is an excellent cup of tea. Nice and strong. It's how I like it."

"I notice," Colin said, "that you haven't come up with any motive for Cornelia and me. Haven't you anything to say about us?"

Welsh cackled again. "I wondered if you'd notice that. If you hadn't, of course, I'd have thought it highly suspicious. Yes, you've an excellent motive, about the best of the lot. I know you've always been on good terms with Staveley, though how you could endure him is something I'll never understand. However, you tend to be on good terms with most people, I know that. You seem to feel there's something to be said in favour of the human race, on which point I beg leave to disagree with you. That isn't what you wanted to discuss, though, is it? Well, my dear Colin, isn't it an obvious thing that although your brother-in-law has an unimpeachable alibi for the time of his wife's death, you haven't? You went to London on an early train, the same train as Staveley. In fact, I believe you travelled together. Then you

met Professor Tierney for lunch. But what were you doing
between the time you arrived at Waterloo and the time you
met the professor?"

"As a matter of fact, I was wandering along Charing
Cross Road, browsing in the bookshops," Colin said. "But I
didn't buy anything and I don't suppose anyone remembers
me."

"So you see, you could have gone to the Tierneys' house,
murdered Mrs. Tierney, then met Professor Tierney for
lunch. And Staveley, who went up on the train with you,
could either have followed you, because for some reason he
was suspicious of you, or he could have been going to see
Mrs. Tierney for his own reasons and happened to see you
go into or come out of the house. So he could have started
his telephone calls to put the fear of God into you. And you
could have recognised his voice, although you pretended
you didn't, and decided to kill him."

Colin nodded thoughtfully. "Yes, it all hangs together, I
have to admit that. But what motive had I for killing poor
Kate?"

"Money, money, money!" Welsh cried with such excitement that he slopped some tea into his saucer. "Of course
you and Tierney arranged it between you. He would inherit
her money and give you a nice slice of it for getting rid of
her, you'd give him an alibi, and no one but a snake like me
would ever suspect you, because we all know you and Cornelia were on excellent terms with her. Now, haven't I made
out a splendid case against you?"

He smiled at Colin, then at Matthew, with the greatest
amity.

"I don't like this conversation," Cornelia said more force-
fully than before. "I think it's dangerous."

"You've no detachment, my dear," Welsh said cheerfully.

"This is simply a logical exercise. Anyway, how could it be dangerous, talking just amongst ourselves?"

"But as soon as you go out, you'll say it all over again to the next person you meet, you know you will," she said. "And even if they don't take you seriously, some of the mud will stick."

"I give you my solemn word, I won't repeat any of it to a soul," he said. "Meanwhile, thank you for letting me chatter. It's done me a lot of good. I can't talk much to Tim. He gets bored and goes out to his workshop. And thank you for the tea. I'll leave you in peace now. I hope the police don't go on bothering you too much."

He got up, gave Cornelia a kiss on the cheek to which she made no response and let himself out of the cottage.

As the door closed on him, Cornelia gave a slight shiver. "He's impossible, isn't he? Why did it have to be someone like him living next door to us instead of a human being? But did you notice, he left out the real motive he might have had for killing Grant? He didn't say a word about it."

"You're thinking of what you told me about his having fallen in love with Kate himself," Matthew said.

She nodded. "It's understandable that he might not want to mention it in front of you; on the other hand, he didn't seem to mind what else he said, did he? So leaving it out was rather—well, noticeable—if one doesn't want to go so far as to say it was suspicious."

"Are you sure about your facts?" Matthew asked. "He really was in love with her?"

"Oh yes, you couldn't help noticing it. He was always dropping in to see her. If she went out, he'd somehow manage to be around and insist on going with her. She used to laugh about it at first, then she got irritated."

Matthew looked at Colin. "Is Cornelia right?"

"I think so," Colin said. "But it's natural he shouldn't

want to talk about it, because he got a complete brush-off. Nobody likes to talk about their humiliations, do they? I don't see anything suspicious in it."

"But if it's true . . ." Matthew began, then paused, gazing before him with a rather vacant expression on his face. "No," he went on absently, "that couldn't have happened."

"I know what you were going to say," Cornelia said. "That he could be a double murderer. He could have killed Kate out of rage because she'd rejected him, then killed Grant because he was the one she'd cared about. And he could have been telephoning us all out of sheer malice."

As she spoke, the telephone rang.

They all started, then looked blankly at it, as if their speaking of it could have conjured up the call. There was a trace of shock on all their faces. Then Colin reached for the telephone and spoke his name into it.

Matthew could hear a voice speaking, though he could not distinguish the words, then Colin said, "Just a moment, he's here," and held the instrument out to Matthew. "For you," he said.

Matthew took it and said, "Tierney speaking."

"This is Superintendent Mellish," a voice said. "We believe we've found the remainder of your wife's jewellery, but we should like you to identify it. Can you come to London tomorrow?"

"Yes, certainly," Matthew replied. "Where did it turn up?"

"In another pawnbroker's in Camden Town."

"Was it taken in by the same girl?"

"I'll tell you about it tomorrow. Eleven-thirty suit you?"

"Eleven-thirty—yes."

Mellish rang off.

Colin and Cornelia were looking at Matthew expectantly. He told them what Mellish had said.

"A pawnbroker again," Colin said. "That doesn't sound much like a professional job. A sneak-thief seems to be the answer. And I should think it makes one thing clear. There can't be any connection between Kate's death and Grant's and we've been rather stupid letting ourselves get half-hypnotised into thinking his death was murder just because hers was. It was accident or suicide. Now I'm going to get ahead with some work, if you don't mind."

He reached for his collection of books and papers and spread them out before him on the table.

Next morning Matthew went to London once more by the eight-three. At Waterloo he took a taxi to his appointment with Mellish. In the past he had always been economical about taxis, but now, he remembered, there was no reason why he should be. He saw Mellish in the same office as before and at once felt the same unreasoning antagonism to him. Matthew knew that it was unreasoning. When he thought the matter over, he realised that Mellish had never been anything but courteous to him and had appeared to be coping with tolerable intelligence with a problem that he took very seriously. But in whatever way the two of them had met, Matthew thought, they would always have felt the same prickly distrust of one another.

The jewellery that had been found at the pawnbroker's in Camden Town was spread out on Mellish's desk when Matthew arrived. He recognised several pieces at once, an amber pendant, a garnet bracelet, a pair of seed pearl earrings, an amethyst necklace. None of it was valuable, though most of it was charming. There were other odds and ends too, some of them mere costume jewellery, of which he was not so sure, because Kate had often bought small things for herself and he had always been lamentably unobservant of such matters. But he was convinced that the collection had belonged to her.

"Yes," he said, "they were hers. I can't swear to them all, but this—and this—and this—" He picked out the pieces of which he was certain. "I remember them clearly."

Mellish gestured to a chair. "Sit down," he said and lowered himself into his own chair behind his desk. He was wearing a different suit today from the one in which Matthew had seen him last, but it had the same look of being a size too small for him, so that his muscles bulged against the fabric. "We've got the man who stole the things, in case you're curious. The same girl took the whole lot to the pawnbroker and her manner made him suspicious, so he got in touch with the police in his area and they happened to know her. She'd been in trouble more than once before and she'd taken the stuff to a pawnbroker much too near her own territory for safety. So it was easy to pick up the man she was living with, and when it turned out he was the milkman who's been coming to your house for the last couple of years, we thought we'd a good enough case and we charged him."

"Charged him—with murder?" Matthew asked with sudden breathlessness.

It seemed incredible that anything could be so simple. The pleasant milkman with whom he had exchanged remarks about the weather almost daily on his way to Welford had broken into the house, stolen Kate's jewellery, been interrupted by her, strangled her and continued on his route. That was all.

Matthew remembered that on the morning of Kate's death he and the milkman had had a brief chat about the unreliability of weather forecasts. Was it possible that the man had already plotted his crime then? Had his friendly face been a mask over horrors? Or had the crime been the result of a sudden impulse, as astonishing to the man himself as to any of his customers?

"Not with murder, no, not yet," Mellish said. "Only with burglary at the moment. He's confessed to that. His story is that he saw you leave when he was up the far end of the street, then when he'd worked his way some distance along it he saw Mrs. Tierney go by, so he knew the house was empty. Then when he took the milk-bottle in to put it on your back doorstep, he noticed the kitchen window was open a few inches and the temptation was too much for him. He pushed the window open, climbed in, looked around for money, didn't find any, then went up to the bedroom, found the jewellery, stuffed it into his pockets and let himself out again, the whole thing taking only a few minutes. Then he went on delivering milk. And that's where the complication comes in."

"You mean when he did this my wife really was away from the house," Matthew said.

Mellish gave a nod of his large head. "And he did go on delivering milk in the normal way. That's been corroborated by a number of people further along the street. By the time Mrs. Tierney came back he was already at the far end of it."

"Mightn't he have finished his route, then come back, remembering that open window?" Matthew suggested.

"But he'd have known Mrs. Tierney might have come back in the interval," Mellish said. "According to his story it was the fact that he knew the house was empty that made him take the risk of going in."

"All the same, he could have come back, rung the bell to see if anyone was in, and if my wife had answered the door, he'd have come up with some yarn to explain why he'd come back. But if for some reason she didn't hear him and didn't come to the door, he might have climbed in, stolen the jewellery and then been surprised by her. And it could be that he murdered her because she knew him. If he'd been a stranger, he could have made off, or knocked her out, and she wouldn't have had much to tell the police. But because she recognised him, she could have ruined his life for him."

Mellish began to tap with two thick fingers on his desk. "I think you like the idea of this man's guilt," he said.

"I have to admit I prefer it to suspecting my wife's friends, which is what I've been doing for the last few days," Matthew said.

Mellish got to his feet. He leant forward towards Matthew with his large face hanging above him like a threat. The antagonism between them was suddenly an almost palpable thing.

"Even though it means you pushed the wrong man off the cliff at Fernley?" Mellish said. "You still prefer it, do you, Professor Tierney?"

Then he sat down again and smiled broadly, as if he had made a good joke.

CHAPTER EIGHT

Matthew was aware only of fury. But anger always made him speechless. He did not try to reply. It was only later, in the train on the way back to Fernley, that he began to think of all the things that he might have said.

And it was only then that he began to feel scared. For the first time he felt as if a net were closing round him. The fact that both Mellish and Drayton seemed to have the same attitude towards him began to seem exceedingly sinister. Not that he believed that they would ever collect enough evidence to be able to arrest him for Grant Staveley's murder. He was not afraid of that. But he found that he was horribly afraid of spending the rest of his life under a cloud of suspicion, of being whispered about for years to come as the man who had been clever enough to get away with it.

A crazy impulse gripped him to jump off the train at the next stop, take the first bus that came along to wherever it was going and go into hiding where no one could find him. People did occasionally disappear successfully. It could be done.

However, the people who disappeared successfully had usually made careful plans in advance and had plenty of money with them or waiting for them somewhere. He had rather less than ten pounds on him. And Colin and Cornelia would of course be upset if he vanished. It would be very callous not to let them know at least that he was alive. And Cornelia was no good at keeping secrets. He had seen something of that recently. And once anyone knew for certain that he was alive, he would soon be tracked down and the suspicions of him would be blacker than ever. . . .

"I do wonder what your religion is," a voice said beside him.

He started and looked round. His inclination was to say that that was a question of which he would like to have notice, but she was far too young for him to say anything of the kind. She looked about seventeen. She was pretty and clean and, to judge by her expression, bewilderingly happy. She had pink, dimpled cheeks, sparkling blue eyes and red hair that shone with brushing and was drawn back from her face with a bright green ribbon, and she was wearing a bright green overcoat with a scarf of sunset hues at her throat. Matthew had been too absorbed in his thoughts to be aware of her until she spoke to him.

"You don't mind my speaking to you, do you?" she said. "I thought you didn't look as if you would and sometimes I can't help speaking to people. There's so much simply bursting inside me, I can't keep it in. I'm going down to our Headquarters, you see, and I get so excited when I go there. The Headquarters of the group I belong to. I've belonged to them for nearly a year and it's completely changed my life."

Matthew had often said hard things about the young in his time, but he was very seldom capable of being unkind to any one of them whom he met face to face. Encountering this girl's radiant cheerfulness, he wondered how many times her life was destined to be completely changed and hoped that each time would bring her as much joy.

"Yes, I used to wear my hair hanging all over my face, really because I wanted to hide, you know," she went on, "and I wore ragged jeans and that. And it's a funny thing but there's a boy in our group who wore his hair down to his shoulders when he joined us, but now he's got it cut quite short and he's shaved off his beard and he says he used to want to hide too, but he doesn't any more."

Matthew was curious what religion it could be that led to the cutting of hair.

"What denomination does your group belong to?" he asked cautiously.

"Oh, we're completely non-sectarian," she answered. "We believe in peace."

"That sounds splendid."

"It is, it's wonderful."

She said it eagerly, as if no one had ever thought of it before, and chattered on while Matthew wondered whether, since he felt so intensely inclined just then to hide rather than to emerge into the open, he might not start by growing his hair and a beard. But it would take time. It would not be of any immediate help to him. He listened gravely to the girl, who took his air of attentiveness for serious interest and as they were drawing into the next station took a notebook out of her handbag, tore out a leaf, wrote something down on it and handed it to him.

"That's the address of our Headquarters," she said. "Do get in touch with us. You'd be so welcome."

She darted towards the door.

An old woman sitting opposite Matthew gave a chuckle.

"She enjoyed that," she said. "It was nice of you to listen to her the way you did. It isn't everyone who'd have the patience."

It intrigued Matthew that the old woman should have seen through him so easily. She was a dumpling of a person with a heavily wrinkled face and several chins. She was wearing an old tweed coat and a head-scarf and had a large collection of parcels, the results of a day's shopping in London, spread out on the table in front of her.

"The young," she said, "they're extraordinary. They think they're finding everything out for the first time."

She then went on to tell Matthew, as pertinaciously as the girl had before her, about the unique discovery of growing old. She told him that she had to go to London twice a year for a check-up at one of the hospitals, and though she did not tell him what her ailment was, he had an impression that it was serious, a fact that she seemed to have faced with equanimity. For her there was no attempt at hiding from what the future was to bring. She had a rock-garden, she told him, which was her great interest in life. By the time that the train reached Fernley, Matthew was wondering why he had ever had his mood of panic, why he had felt such a claustrophobic sense of enclosure in his own problems that there had seemed to be no answer for him but flight.

He walked from the station to the Naylors' cottage. On the way, walking along Fernley's one street of shops, he passed one that had the name "R. Staveley" over the door. The window was filled with oddments of pottery, chains of beads, paperbacks, water-colours of the village and the coast, certainly not by Grant Staveley, and jars of local honey. On an impulse Matthew went to the door. He wanted all of a sudden to talk to Rachel Staveley. But a notice hanging inside the glass panel in the door said that the shop was closed. He continued on his way to the cottage.

However, when he reached it, he went past it to the white house higher up the hill. Turning in at the gate, he went up to the door, rang the bell and stood there wondering how he was to explain precisely why he had come when he himself was not sure of it. The door was opened almost at once by Eleanor. Close behind her, as if he were there to protect her against some possibly dangerous intruder, was Tim Welsh.

They both fell back when they saw Matthew and Eleanor
surprised him by giving him a rather pleased smile.

"We thought perhaps you were the police back again,"
she said. "Is it Mummy you want? She's gone to sit on the
bench outside. We've been trying to get her to come in. It
isn't the weather for sitting out there. She'll catch cold. But
she doesn't listen. She sits there staring out to sea as if she's
watching for a ship coming in. Do you think you could get
her to come in, Professor Tierney? She really ought to."

Matthew could not think of any reason why he should
have any influence with Rachel Staveley, but he agreed that
it was not a day for sitting out of doors. It was still and
clammy and even colder than the last few days. Winter was
still doggedly fending off the coming spring.

Eleanor took him into a large, light sitting room. Its window took up nearly the whole of one wall and faced towards the sea, a sea as grey and cheerless-looking as the
sky. The room was a white and black one. There were white
walls, a near-white carpet and curtains that matched it, slim
Scandinavian chairs with black corduroy cushions, one or
two thick black rugs and a big black bowl filled with white
daffodils standing on a table in the window. The only colour in the room was in the pictures, all Grant Staveleys,
which blazed with orange and red and yellow round the
walls.

Eleanor saw Matthew looking at one of them and remarked, "Tim says we ought to get them insured. They're
sure to go up in value."

Compared with the girl who had wept in her mother's
arms the day before, she sounded remarkably composed.

"Well, he was just beginning to become successful," Tim
said. "These may be worth thousands in a few years' time."

"I've got one of his paintings, you know," Matthew said.
"He painted my wife."

"I know," Eleanor said. "It wasn't one of his good ones. She was much too lovely for him to paint. He was much better at painting ugly people, though he always said they weren't ugly if you knew how to look at them. But beautiful people bored him."

"Did you think Kate was beautiful?" Matthew asked.

"Oh, she was fabulous!" she said enthusiastically.

"Did he ever paint you?"

"Over and over again and I got rather tired of it. For one thing, they all came out looking like Mummy, not like me."

"You are rather alike," Matthew said.

"Not as much as all that. It was dull too, sitting still for hours when I'd sooner have been doing other things."

"Such as what?"

She shrugged her shoulders. "Oh, all sorts of things. Earning some money for myself. I don't like being dependent."

Tim put an arm round her. "And getting married to me. And I was going to teach her about the antique business. She started going to sales with me. She's got quite a good eye. And she's good in the shop too. She's clever with customers. But Grant put a stop to all that."

"I suppose you could just have gone away if you'd really wanted to," Matthew said.

The girl flushed faintly. Moving away from Tim's encircling arm, she said, "But there was Mummy. It would have worried her if I'd left."

"It's what you'll do now, though, isn't it?" Matthew asked.

"Of course," Tim said.

"I think so," she corrected him. "I haven't really thought anything out since yesterday."

"That hasn't really changed things," Tim said. "Not between you and me."

"No, I know." But there was a note of uncertainty in her voice. Matthew thought that perhaps she had had an over-dose of dominant males and that if Tim pressed her too hard it might bring about the very thing that Grant Stave-ley had tried to achieve, the breakdown of the relationship between them. She went on, "The night before last, when Mummy and Grant had been quarrelling about me and I couldn't stand it any more, I went out to Tim and we went for a drive and we decided we'd go away together and get married at once. We meant to go next day—that was yester-day. Then of course we couldn't. And now I've got the feel-ing we ought to wait. There's no reason for hurry any more and, as I said, there's Mummy to think of. But you're going out to see her now, aren't you? Come out through the garden."

She went to the big window and opened a glass door in the middle of it.

Matthew stepped out into the garden. In two straight rows the borders filled with white daffodils reached to the garden wall. He walked down the strip of grass between them and out through the gate that opened on to the cliff path.

He saw Rachel sitting on the bench. She was in her rain-coat and had a scarf tied over her short, fair hair. She was sitting hunched up, her hands thrust deep into her pockets and the collar of the raincoat turned up about her ears. She was gazing out to sea as if she were watching for something of deep importance to her to come to her out of the distant greyness. Was it her husband she expected to see rise up above the edge of the cliff? She gave no sign of hearing Matthew approach until he was almost beside her, then she looked up at him with a wan smile. He thought that she had probably been aware of him from the time that he had opened the garden gate.

"I thought you'd gone to London," she said in her soft, level voice.

"I went this morning." He gestured at the bench. "May I sit down?"

"Of course." She moved a little way along the bench to make more room for him.

"How did you know I'd gone?" he asked.

"Cornelia came in to see how I was," she answered. "She's very kind. And she told me you'd gone. She said the police had sent for you."

"Yes, they'd found my wife's jewellery and wanted me to identify it."

"Does that mean they've found the man who stole it?"

"Yes."

"And is he . . . ?" She stopped. She turned her head to look at him directly. Her pale face was pinched with the cold. "Cornelia says you're terribly depressed. She says the police are bothering you."

"You were going to ask if this man's Kate's murderer, weren't you?" Matthew said. "Well, he may be, but there are complications. He's our milkman and he admits he got into the house when Kate and I were out of it and stole the jewellery. But by the time Kate got home from shopping he was a long way off, down the other end of the street. I did my best to convince myself he must have come back and done the murder, but the police don't believe it and I can't honestly say, now that I've thought it over, that I believe it myself."

"But why are the police bothering you?" she asked. "You've got an alibi for the whole day it happened, haven't you?"

"They aren't bothering me about Kate's murder," Matthew said.

"Well, then?"

He moved uneasily on the bench. The cold was biting through his overcoat. It was not as warm as his quilted anorak.

"The reason I came to see you this afternoon," he said, "is that I want to know if you believe I killed your husband. The police both here and in London seem to think I did and for some reason it began to feel extraordinarily important to me to find out if you did too. So I'm just asking you, do you believe it?"

She gave a faintly ironic smile.

"If I did, do you think I'd admit it, sitting out here alone with you, with no one to see if you pushed me out after Grant?"

"Oh, you needn't worry about that. Eleanor and Tim know that I came out to see you. If anything unfortunate should happen to you, I'd be suspected at once."

"You reassure me." There was mockery in her voice. "But why is it important what I think?"

"I'm not sure. But I don't seem to mind too much what anyone else thinks."

"Even the police?"

"Least of all the police. As individuals they don't mean anything to me, and if it came to charging me with murder, I don't think they'd have any case at all. That man Mellish in London scared me for a bit, but I've calmed down now. He thinks my motive was that I believed your husband killed my wife and I was taking revenge on him, and there's a bit of confusion about a walking-stick of mine they found here on this bench, and they know I came out for a walk up this way that evening. But I doubt if they could convince a jury with that."

"They asked me about the walking-stick," she said. "They asked if Grant took it to the Naylors' house the other evening and I told them he did." Then in an emotionless tone that made Matthew wonder what had happened to her in the past to drain all normal animation out of her, she added, "Do you think Grant killed Kate?"

"I thought so at first," he admitted. "I guessed she'd fallen in love with him. It wasn't that she ever said much about him, but there was the curious business of the white flowers. After her visit here, when she met him, she wouldn't have any flowers but white ones in the house, and then I saw your white daffodils here. It was rather a long shot, but it seemed clear to me she was trying to do something that would make her feel identified with him. But she didn't get anywhere with it with him, did she? He never fell in love with her."

She drew a hand out of her pocket and sketched an almost apologetic gesture with it.

"It's true he had a thing about white flowers and she copied him, I suppose to try to impress him. But you haven't answered my question."

"Do I think Grant killed Kate? The truth is, I've never been able to think of a good reason why he should have."

"So you don't still think he did."

"I'm not sure, but—no, I suppose not."

"She wasn't important to him, you know. He showed that in that picture he painted of her, didn't he? There's a dreadful contempt in it."

"Yet she liked it."

"Oh no, she didn't," she said positively. "I was there when he gave it to her and I saw the look of intense hurt on her face. But she was much too proud to admit it. She pretended to see something very profound in it, said no one but Grant had ever understood her so wonderfully and worked really hard at convincing herself she liked it. But she hated it, because it showed her as a shallow, foolish woman, not simply the very beautiful one that she was used to people seeing. But she'd have died sooner than let anyone see that."

"She did die," Matthew said.

Colour swept into her cheeks. "I'm sorry, I didn't mean . . ."

"I know you didn't. But I'm wondering if what you're telling me is that by the end Kate hated Grant."

"She may have, I don't know. But that still wouldn't have given him a reason for killing her."

"Unless—it's the only thing I've been able to think of— she'd found out something about him that she was using against him. If she'd started to hate him, she might have done that."

She shook her head. "He wasn't a man with secrets. He'd have been very hard to blackmail. He liked everyone to be very well informed about his worst qualities and actions. He was more than a bit of an exhibitionist about them. That's to say, except . . ." She paused again and gave him another quick look. "Have you been listening to Ambrose Welsh talking about him?"

"I've heard him talk a good deal," Matthew said.

"And he's been telling you that Grant and Eleanor were in love with one another, and you think that's what Kate could have been holding over him." There was more life in her voice than Matthew had heard before, given to it by an undercurrent of anger. "Of course it isn't true. Eleanor's in love with Tim. She was very fond of Grant, but that began when she was a child and it was absolutely innocent. Ambrose has a foul mind and loves spreading scandal."

"But what about Grant's feeling for her?" Matthew asked.

She took longer to answer this time. "If I try to tell you the truth, you'll say it's altogether too complicated," she said. "You'll say I imagined it all. But I told you, d'you remember, that Grant and I were in love with each other when we were children? I don't think anyone's ever mattered to me quite as much as he did then, and I think that may have been true of him. Then we were separated for years. I married and it was a really happy marriage. Tony was as unlike Grant as anyone could be. He was a very honest, very gentle, reliable man with a great deal of humour and no self-assertiveness. He was very practical too and perfectly happy if he had straightforward, practical problems to deal with. Then he was killed and I had to start earning a living while I was looking after Eleanor, so I thought I'd take a shop, because I could have her there with me while I was at work, and I happened to read an advertisement of the shop here being for sale, and I managed to raise a mortgage and moved in and gradually began to cope with life again. And then one day in walked Grant. He'd come in to buy a paperback he'd seen in the window and we recognised one another at once and three months later we were married. But I've always thought he wanted to marry me because of Eleanor. As soon as he saw her he said she was exactly like what I'd been as a child. Do you understand what I'm trying to say? I don't think he wanted simply to be a father to her. I think he was trying to get back to that old daydream of ours when we were children."

"And you?" Matthew said. "Did you marry him for the sake of the same daydream and find it had died on you? Because it did die, didn't it?"

"Oh yes. D'you know, sitting out here alone, I haven't been thinking of Grant, I've been thinking of Tony. I've been going through losing him all over again. You'd think that would tear me to pieces, but there's a sort of quiet in it. All these last few years Grant's been between him and me. I tried to be fair to Grant, you see. I knew I'd married him for the wrong reasons, just as he had me, and I tried to stick to my side of the bargain. I'd married him partly because he

was so fond of Eleanor and I thought she ought to have a father, and partly out of sheer loneliness. That's a very
different thing from love, though just how little I loved him
wasn't a thing I realised until some time later. And by then
Eleanor had become very dependent on him and I didn't
think it was the time to snatch her away from him. And
the right time never seemed to come."

"You'll have to face that loneliness again now," Matthew
said.

She nodded, her gaze back on the hazy distance. "I'll
find it peaceful."

"You may miss Grant far more than you expect."

"Oh, I miss him already in all kinds of ways. One gets
accustomed to things. Don't you miss Kate?"

"Yes," he said, "more than I expected."

"Yet you didn't love her very much, did you?"

"Things didn't work out somehow. But they began well. I
don't know what went wrong."

"I don't think things do go wrong, you know, unless
they're wrong from the start and then there's no putting
them right. The mistake comes right at the beginning in
one's ignorance of oneself. What are you going to do now
that you're alone?"

"Sell the house, get a flat, go on with my job."

"I haven't thought ahead as far as that. I'll sell the house,
I suppose. If Eleanor marries Tim and moves out to live
with him, it would be far too big for me. I could offer it to
them, of course, but I've a feeling that if I do they'll feel
they've got to ask me to live with them and I don't want
that. After the way Grant and Ambrose have muddied the
waters for them, I want them to be as free of interfering relatives as they possibly can."

"I don't see you being interfering," Matthew said.

"But I'd be there, and there should be no one there to

watch you when you start trying to create your new life. You need all the freedom you can get."

"Are you sure they're going to marry?" Matthew asked. "When I was talking to her just now I thought Eleanor was showing signs of uncertainty."

She shook her head. "No, she's very much in love with Tim. But at the moment she's in a state of shock. She's completely confused. She loved Grant very much, then she made up her mind to defy him—she told me she and Tim had made up their minds to go away together—then Grant died and she's overwhelmed with guilt, as if she were somehow responsible for it. But that won't last long. And I think the best thing would be for them to find a small flat or cottage of their own and for me to sell the house. I think I'll sell the shop too and start up something new somewhere else. If I sell the house and the shop I shan't be pressed for money for some time."

"I've had an invitation to go to Australia for a year," Matthew said. "I'm thinking of accepting it."

She was silent for a moment, then gave a nod. "I'd do that, if I were you. It sounds a wonderful place to disappear into, if you want to lick your wounds."

He looked away from her and, like her, settled his gaze on the cloudy horizon.

"Do you still believe Grant committed suicide?" he asked.

"I never believed it," she said.

"Then why did you say you did?"

"Because I was afraid that Eleanor was involved in his death. I didn't believe at first it could be an accident, he knew this path so well. And his having left his stick carefully here on this bench made suicide seem plausible. And I was so afraid. . . . You see, that evening when Grant and I quarrelled I saw Eleanor suddenly turn white and she left the room and I heard the front door slam. I thought, she's going to Tim. Then it was hours before she came back and she was in a strange mood—I'd call it excited and frightened. So when we found Grant on the rocks next day, I thought she knew what had happened. I thought there must have been a struggle between him and Tim on the path and Tim had pushed him over and Eleanor had seen it. Tim wouldn't have done it intentionally, I know, but in the rain and the darkness anything could have happened."

"And what makes you think now that that isn't what happened?"

She did not answer. The silence lengthened out between them. A gull flew down near them, crying at them with a sound of anger.

"Is it because you think I'm a better suspect?" Matthew asked.

She gave a sharp shiver, stood up abruptly and pulled her coat closely about her.

"It must have been an accident," she said. "What else could it have been? He was angry, he'd drunk too much, it was dark. He lost his head and he lost his way."

"Leaving the walking-stick here?"

"That doesn't mean anything." She turned to look him straight in the eyes with a long stare. Her own eyes, he noticed for the first time, were not blue like her daughter's, but a deep shade of grey with a very dark rim round the iris. "If I were you, Matthew, I'd go on believing it was an accident and I'd go on believing it was the milkman who murdered Kate and I'd go to Australia and I'd make a new life for myself. That's what I'm going to do. I'm going to make a new life for myself. Somehow."

She moved past him swiftly to the gate in the wall, crossed the lawn to the house and disappeared.

Matthew stood up and started along the path to the Naylors' cottage. He was thinking of how, each time that he had asked her if she suspected him of her husband's murder, she had avoided giving him a direct answer. That seemed to indicate that she did suspect him. But either she did not want him to suffer for it, because in her heart she was glad to be rid of Staveley, or she was afraid, out there alone on the cliffs with a murderer, of what he might feel driven to do. Or could it mean that she knew who the murderer was? Had Tim and Eleanor between them been guilty after all? Had she seen the murder committed? It did not seem impossible.

He found Colin and Cornelia in the living room of the cottage, both nursing drinks. The room was warm and bright, with the curtains drawn already, the lights turned on and a big log smouldering in the grate.

"Well, how did it go?" Colin asked, getting up to make a drink for Matthew.

"The business of the jewellery?" Matthew said, taking a chair by the fire. "It was Kate's. And they've got the man who stole it. Our milkman, who's been coming to us every day for a couple of years. I've had a chat with him almost every morning when I left home. He seemed an ordinary, decent sort of chap and I'd find the whole thing hard to believe except that he's confessed."

"Confessed he killed Kate?" Cornelia exclaimed in astonishment.

"No, just to the theft." Matthew went on to explain why it seemed more than doubtful that the milkman had committed the murder. "D'you know, I've got a feeling we may never discover who murdered Kate," he added.

"Why not?" Colin asked.

"Because I don't think we've even begun to think of it in the right way. I've been obsessed with Staveley and the police have been obsessed with their burglar. But I never managed to think up a good reason why Staveley should have murdered Kate and the police don't think their burglar, now that they've got him, could have had anything to do with the job. All that they can think of is that I probably murdered Staveley because I thought he'd killed Kate. And I know they're wrong about that, even if nobody else does."

Cornelia frowned at him. "You're getting at something, but I'm not sure what."

"I'm not sure myself, but I've got a sort of feeling. . . ." Matthew tipped his glass this way and that, watching the whisky swirl in it. "You see, I found out something this evening that may be relevant."

"Go on," Colin said.

"Well, I found out that neither Eleanor nor Tim has an alibi for the time of Staveley's death."

"But Ambrose said Tim was with him that evening."

"Yes, but it isn't true. I've just been up to the Staveleys'—"

"Why?" Cornelia interrupted.

"I felt I had to find out if Rachel thought I'd killed her husband. It seemed important, somehow, to find out what people are saying."

"Just people, or Rachel in particular?" she inquired.

"I suppose I should say Rachel in particular," he admitted.

"And does she?" Colin asked.

"I shouldn't be surprised. But she and I happen to be in almost identical positions. Whatever she thinks, she's got some sympathy for me, and I don't think she'll try to work up a case against me unless Eleanor and Tim get into trouble."

"I don't understand this thing about Eleanor and Tim," Cornelia said.

"Well, Eleanor told me that when her mother and Staveley had their quarrel about her before he went out of the house and disappeared, she went out and got Tim and they went for a drive and had a long talk and decided to go away and get married. So Tim wasn't with his father for most of the evening, and he and Eleanor could have met Staveley on the path after they got back—"

"But—but—" Cornelia broke in excitedly, "don't you understand what that means? The person who hasn't got an alibi is Ambrose! Tim doesn't matter. He'd never harm anybody. But Ambrose is an altogether different kind. And he deliberately lied to us about it. He dragged in the fact that Tim had been at home with him that evening. Matthew, I think you've stumbled on something very important and we've got to do something about it. And I know exactly what!"

CHAPTER NINE

She reached for the telephone.

Colin's hand shot out and caught her wrist. "What are you going to do?"

"Ring up Ambrose."

"What are you going to say?"

"Just wait and see."

"No," Colin said. "We've got to think this over." He turned to Matthew. "What do you think about it?"

"I haven't thought anything much about it yet," Matthew said. "But Cornelia's right, Welsh hasn't an alibi and he did lie to us."

"To protect himself or to protect Tim?" Colin asked.

"Your guess is as good as mine. Is it possible they were both in it together?"

Colin looked back at Cornelia. "What's your idea?"

She smiled. "You don't suppose I was going to ring up and say, 'Oh, by the way, did you murder Grant?'" She reached for the telephone again.

"No," Colin repeated. "Let's talk this over before we do anything. What were you going to say?"

"My idea," she said, "was to set a trap for him."

"How?"

"I was going to disguise my voice," she said, "and just say I saw him push Grant off the cliff and I wanted a thousand pounds for it and I'd meet him at his garden gate in an hour's time to collect it. And you and Matthew can go and hide yourselves up there and if Ambrose comes to the gate you can come out and say we know he's guilty. And if he doesn't come you can probably write him off."

"He might come out of sheer curiosity," Colin said.

"And even if he's guilty," Matthew said, "he might think the best thing to do was to telephone the police and tell them about the call."

"That wouldn't do any harm. They wouldn't be able to trace it." Cornelia gave a little bounce of frustration in her chair. "Oh, do let's get on with it, or have you some better idea?"

"I think it's a better idea to do nothing," Colin said.

"And let him get away with it?"

"We could tell the police about his false alibi and leave the rest to them. It's their job."

"If I was a blackmailer," Matthew said, "I wouldn't arrange to meet a man who'd probably committed a murder or two on that cliff path in the dark. It would make a third murder a little too easy for him."

"But that's part of my plan," she said. "He'll realise how vulnerable the blackmailer will be, particularly since it's a woman's voice he'll hear on the telephone, and he'll be tempted out to deal with her. Then in fact he'll find the two of you."

Colin shook his head, but he was beginning to look undecided. And he was too used to letting Cornelia have her way to hold out for long against her.

"He'll recognise your voice," he said dubiously, in what sounded like a last attempt to dissuade her. "He'll simply laugh at you."

"Then we can pretend it was just a joke, can't we?"

"A pretty macabre sort of joke," Matthew said. He wanted no part of her plan.

"My guess is," Colin said, "if he doesn't recognise your

voice, he'll come straight round to tell us how he's just been rung up by our anonymous caller."

"And that won't do any harm," she said, "because naturally we shan't know anything about it."

"Well, let's hear that disguised voice of yours first."

She saw that she had won her point and laughed as if she were beginning to enjoy the thought of some play-acting.

"You begin by putting a handkerchief over the telephone and speaking through it," she said. "I've often read that in detective stories. It makes it sound as if you've got a cold. Then—ought I to go shrill or gruff and deep, d'you think? I think going high would be easier. Then perhaps a bit of an accent. . . ." She stopped, gave the telephone a frowning look as if she suspected it of playing a trick on her, and said, "I can't do it."

"Thank the Lord for that," Colin said.

"You put me out," she said. "If you hadn't stopped me I would have gone straight ahead and done it, but now I feel self-conscious. I'd make a mess of it."

"Anyway, Welsh won't have a thousand pounds in the house," Matthew said. "He'd tell you he couldn't meet you with it in an hour."

"D'you think that would have been asking too much, then?" she asked. "Would five hundred pounds have been better?"

"I'm afraid I don't know much about the current rates in blackmail," he answered.

"Don't you think asking for too little would be suspicious?"

"The whole thing's suspicious," Colin said. "Now let's forget about it and see if we can think of something more practical."

She sighed, picked up the drink that she had put down and turned her head to gaze into the fire. Her gaze grew abstracted, dreamy, almost drowsy. Colin and Matthew fell silent too. The only sounds in the room were the little crackling and hissing sounds of the flames that licked around the smouldering log.

Matthew felt extraordinarily tired. He could easily have let himself fall asleep. The day during which he had gone to London, recognised Kate's jewellery, been accused of murder, met the ardent girl whose life had been changed so much for the better and the old woman whose life was almost certainly coming to an end and who knew it, then had talked with Eleanor and Tim and then with Rachel out in the cold, high above the rhythmically pounding surf, seemed to stretch out endlessly behind him. But it was not only today that had been too long. All the days since Kate's death seemed to have been squeezed out of shape into long, fragile threads of time tangled together and past his power to unravel.

All that time he had felt tired. He felt that there had never been a time in his life when he had not felt tired. Was it that he felt more grief than he realised, or perhaps even more fear for himself? Or was it just middle age assaulting him suddenly, springing upon him unexpectedly, taking him by the throat and shaking all resistance out of him? He had often noticed that people aged by fits and starts, not in any smooth, gradual way. Something happened to them and without warning they became several years older than they had been a few weeks before, and they never recovered the lost ground. Had that happened to him?

He found himself thinking of Rachel, sitting crouched on the bench, waiting for something, even if it was only an image or a memory, to come to her out of the depths.

He would have liked to know her better, he thought, if only everything had been different for them both. They shared a fate so similar that it might have brought them together if they had not both been too full of distrust to let anyone come close. She seemed a quiet, tranquil, gentle woman, with more understanding than he was used to encountering. Kate had been none of those things. At her best she had had the intense charm of overflowing vitality, linked to beauty, which could sweep you along in uncritical delight, and at her worst she had been querulous, selfish and rather a bore. That had been the combination of qualities which he had been accustomed to living with, so accustomed that unconsciously he half-expected to meet them everywhere, and when he did not, hardly knew how to act. If he wanted to know Rachel better, he realised, he would have to make some serious readjustments in himself, change some habits of thought, start in some things almost from the beginning. But was that possible for a man beginning to feel the weariness of middle age?

Cornelia moved swiftly. Before Colin or Matthew had realised what she was going to do, she was back at the telephone and was dialling rapidly. As she did so she mumbled to herself, as if she were rehearsing something that she had in her mind, that she must not forget.

Matthew heard the ringing sound end and a man's voice speak.

She clapped a fold of her handkerchief over the mouthpiece and in a thin, high, old-woman's voice, quite unlike her own and with one of the most unconvincing cockney accents that Matthew had ever heard, said, "I saw you give him that push and I want a thousand pounds or I'll go to the police. Bring it to your garden gate at eight o'clock tomorrow night. Eight—tomorrow."

The man's voice exclaimed, asked some question, rose in excitement, then was cut off as Cornelia quietly put the telephone down. She looked round at Colin and Matthew with a smile of satisfaction.

"Well?" she said.

"What did he say?" Colin asked, sounding nervous and exasperated.

"He didn't laugh."

"But what did he say?"

"You said he'd laugh, but he didn't."

"Oh, my God . . . !" Colin burst out with a rare sound of anger. "I asked you—"

"Yes, yes, and he didn't say anything of any importance," she answered. "He just asked me who the hell I thought I was, which was quite natural in the circumstances, then I cut him off. And I gave him till tomorrow to get the money, so he can do something about it if he's got anything on his conscience."

"What will you bet he'll be round here in ten minutes to tell us all about it," Colin said.

She shook her head. "I'm not a betting woman, but I think you're wrong. Now I'd better get on with some cooking."

She went out to the kitchen.

Ten minutes passed, twenty, thirty, and Ambrose Welsh did not come to the cottage.

In the morning both Colin and Cornelia were in an unusual mood. They seemed not to be speaking to one another. Colin looked sullen and tight-lipped, Cornelia was making an unnecessary amount of noise as she moved around, banging crockery down on the table with uncontrolled violence and avoiding looking in Colin's direction. She also avoided looking at Matthew. He recognised that they must have had a quarrel the night before and thought what a remarkable thing it was that this was something that he had never witnessed before. He and Cornelia had had their quarrelsome childhood and he had gone on regarding her ever since as a naturally quarrelsome person, but he had never seen Colin seriously angry before. It was anger, Matthew supposed, that was the matter with Colin now, anger about her preposterous telephone call, which he had not wanted her to make, and now they were both sulking.

The unfamiliar tension in the atmosphere drove Matthew out of the cottage earlier than he had intended, hoping that they would have made their peace before he returned. If Colin and Cornelia were to start falling out with one another, then what human relationship was safe? Matthew was on Colin's side in the disagreement. He had thought Cornelia's call ridiculous. But he was thankful that neither of them seemed to expect his support. Taking the road down the hill, he strolled into the village.

Finding himself after a few minutes looking into the window of an antique shop, he remembered that he wanted to buy Cornelia a present in return for the walking-stick that she had given him, even though this had not brought him much luck. He went into the shop. It was the same as a thousand other antique shops, small, dark, cluttered, though less dusty than some and relying for its trade on an assortment of Victorian knick-knacks, objects that Matthew was a little too old to think of as being really antique, remembering their like, as he did, in the homes of various grandaunts. But there was a Georgian bureau which he guessed was of fairly high quality, a sofa table of some grace, and one or two other objects which he imagined would turn out to be surprisingly expensive. The bell over the door chimed as he entered the shop and Tim Welsh appeared in a doorway that led to a room behind it.

"Oh, are you looking for my father?" he said when he saw Matthew. "I'm afraid he isn't here."

He was in a thick sweater with the sleeves pushed up and smears of sawdust on it and had a curly woodshaving caught in his hair.

"If you don't mind, I just wanted to look round," Matthew said. "I want to buy a present for Cornelia."

"Go ahead." For a moment Tim seemed to be about to turn back into the room from which he had just emerged, leaving Matthew to look round by himself, but then he lingered, staying silently watching as Matthew began to scrutinize the jugs, vases, bowls, blank-faced Staffordshire dogs and Toby jugs on the shelves that lined the room. After a little while Tim blurted out, "If all you want is to ask me questions of some sort, you don't have to buy anything, you know."

"No, I really should like to find something for Cornelia," Matthew said. "She's been very good to me."

He did not add that he thought a present might help to restore her good temper, which would be satisfactory for him as well as for Colin.

"But don't you want to ask me anything?" Tim went on.

"No, should I?" Matthew said. "What about?"

"About that alibi of mine."

"I'm not the police," Matthew answered. "It's not my business."

"I can explain it," Tim said. "Eleanor and I told the police the truth, you see, and then discovered my father had said he and I had been at home all the evening. So then he changed his story and told the police the truth too and they seemed to accept it. That man Drayton seems to be fairly reasonable."

"When was this?" Matthew asked.

"This morning."

"Your father told the police this morning that he'd been alone the evening Staveley was killed?"

"Yes. Of course he'd have been wiser to tell them the truth in the first place, but he was worried about Eleanor and me. You don't know him. He's wonderfully good-natured, even if he doesn't sound it, but he hasn't got much common sense."

"Did anything special happen to make him decide to tell the truth?" Matthew asked.

"Not that I know of," Tim said. "We talked it over and came to the conclusion it would be the best thing to do."

So it looked as if Ambrose Welsh had not told Tim anything about Cornelia's telephone call of the evening before, which, it seemed, had made Welsh decide to put himself into the hands of the police rather than into the clutches of a blackmailer. Perhaps he had more common sense than his son gave him credit for.

Matthew picked up a bowl from the shelf in front of him. It was white, with a dark blue rim and touches of gold.

"What's this?" he asked.

"It's Caughley—thirty-nine pounds," Tim replied.

Matthew quickly put the bowl down again and moved further along the room.

In the end he bought a Hilditch cream jug for five pounds. It had gay little Chinese-looking figures painted on it and some sprays of bright flowers that made the ladies with their parasols look as if they had strayed into an English garden. It would look quite well, he thought, with the other china on the dresser in the Naylors' living room. All the time that he was in the shop he felt Tim watching him uneasily, as if he felt sure that Matthew had come into the shop for some purpose besides buying a piece of china, and when Matthew left without having asked him any more questions the boy seemed almost perturbed.

When Matthew arrived back at the cottage he found, to his relief, that the atmosphere had become normal. Cornelia received the cream jug with appropriate exclamations of pleasure and gratitude and put it on one of the shelves of the dresser. But she also gave him a shrewd glance.

"So you've been talking to Tim," she said.

"Yes, and your trap isn't going to work," he told her. "He told me Welsh got in touch with the police this morning and told them the truth about having no alibi. He claimed he'd lied because he was worried about Eleanor and Tim."

"That was cunning of him," she said. "Now I suppose it would be a waste of time to go out to meet him this evening. He won't come."

"I always thought it would be a waste of time," Colin said. "He wouldn't have come in any case."

It seemed to stimulate her contradictoriness. "It might be as well to make sure."

"If it's of any interest," Matthew said, "my impression is that he's said nothing to Tim about that call of yours. He didn't know why his father had decided to come clean with the police this morning."

"That *is* interesting," she said. "Perhaps we ought to go, just to see what happens."

"We?" Colin said sharply. "You're coming too, are you? All three of us are going? We're going to lay on a reception committee?"

"Not if you don't want me to," she answered peaceably. "But you and Matthew should go."

"And suppose he does come out to meet us," Colin said, "what do we do then? Apologize for having played a bad joke?"

Cornelia rested her head on one hand and considered the question. After a moment she said, "You can always fall back on that, if you have to. But you know Ambrose—if he runs into trouble with anyone, he takes the initiative. He'll give you a lead himself."

"What do you think about it, Matthew?" Colin asked.

"To tell the truth, I'm rather in favour of going now,"

Matthew said. "I wasn't until I'd talked to Tim, but now
that I know Welsh told him nothing about the call, I'm sure
that means he took it seriously. I think it scared him. That
may not have anything to do with Staveley's death, but it
would be interesting to find out why he's frightened."

"All right, if that's how you feel," Colin said with a sigh,
then picked up a book and made it plain he wanted to
withdraw from the discussion.

It was about ten minutes to eight when he and Matthew,
both wearing their anoraks, set off together up the cliff path.
Colin cursed quietly when they discovered that it was beginning to rain again. It was only light rain, but enough to
make them pull up their hoods. Matthew let Colin lead the
way. He knew what he was making for. This turned out to
be a clump of stunted hawthorns close to the wall beside the
Welshes' gate. Leafless and with only a few dried berries
clinging to them, in daylight they would not have provided
any cover, but now it was enough to stand among them to
become invisible. Colin thrust his way in between two of the
bushes, muttering sullenly as twigs whipped against his face,
and Matthew moved in beside him, shivering slightly in the
clamminess of the night.

He did not feel sure why they were hiding. There did not
seem to be much point in it, unless the truth was that Colin
did not intend that they should be seen at all, even if Ambrose Welsh did come to his gate. To see whether or not he
came was in fact the interesting question. Showing themselves and speaking to him would not wring any admissions
from him. He would say the obvious thing, that he had
merely come to find out who had made the outrageous call
the evening before, and that might truly be his only reason
for coming.

Matthew began to wonder why he had ever thought
Cornelia's plan a good one and to wish that he and Colin

had not come. He almost suggested that they should not wait. Eight o'clock came and passed. Except for the beating of the surf at the foot of the cliffs and the very faint pattering of the rain the night was silent. Silent as the tomb, he caught himself suddenly thinking. Silent as death. And the fancy took him that he could smell death in the dankness of the night air. Perhaps after all a murderer would presently walk out to meet them.

A light footstep sounded on the path inside the garden. He felt Colin catch him by the arm and hold him tight. Then the footsteps stopped. Whoever it was had paused some yards before reaching the gate. Then after a moment the footsteps came on again, faster now, as if some hesitation had been overcome. The gate creaked and Rachel Staveley walked out on to the path.

It was just light enough to see who it was.

"Well?" she said in a clear voice, looking round. "Where are you?"

Colin gave Matthew a slight push. With water shaken from the branches of the bushes spraying his face, he emerged from them on to the path. It took him a moment to realise that Colin was remaining where he was. But that was best. Whatever was to happen now, it was a good thing that there should be a witness.

Rachel was wearing her raincoat, with the usual scarf over her hair. With his eyes accustomed to the darkness, Matthew could see her features clearly, as set as a mask, but it was impossible to see colour in her face. Her mouth was a dark gash, her eyes were circles of shadow. She stood very still as he approached, watching him. He could not read her expression.

Both of them were silent as they met, neither of them willing to speak. Matthew could think of nothing to say. She was the first to grow tired of waiting.

"So it was Cornelia," she said. "I didn't believe it at first."

"Cornelia?" he said, trying to act as if he did not know what she meant.

"On the telephone last night," she said impatiently. "Ambrose said he recognised her voice at once. She so overdid the business of disguising it that he guessed who it was immediately."

"That doesn't explain what you're doing here," he said.

"I came to tell you not to play these silly games. They're no help to anyone. But of course I expected Cornelia herself."

"But it was Welsh she telephoned. How do you come into it?"

"He rang me up after her call and asked me what I thought he ought to do."

"I didn't know you were such good friends," Matthew said.

"We aren't specially good friends," she answered.

"Then why did he choose you to tell about the call?"

"I think after his fashion he trusts me, as far as he's capable of trusting anyone."

"And what did you say to him?"

"What was obvious—that Cornelia was so afraid you were going to be suspected of Grant's murder that she was floundering around, trying to fix the guilt somewhere else. Finding that Ambrose hadn't got an alibi made her feel sure she'd found the answer to her problem. It's very loyal of her, but it's stupid."

"Why? Suppose she's found the right answer. Suppose it's you who's being just a bit stupid, Rachel."

"I told you, Grant's death was an accident," she said incisively.

"You've no proof of that."

"You've no proof it was murder."

"But if it was, what's wrong with Welsh as a suspect?"

She made a curious sound, a small, muted sound of desperation.

"But can't you understand, Matthew, Cornelia's right in her way?" she said. "If the police make up their minds it was murder, then they're bound to suspect you. You told them yourself you believed Grant murdered your wife, and if that isn't a good motive for killing him, what is? So when I say Cornelia's stupid, all I mean is she shouldn't act as if she took for granted his death was murder. That's only going to do you harm. She should say what I do now, that it was an accident."

He wished that he could make out some expression on the pale blur of her face.

"I wonder what you really believe," he said. "Do you realise you still haven't told me?"

"Does it matter?"

"Only that it's puzzling, if you think I'm such a good suspect, why you should seem to be trying to help me."

She did not answer.

When he had waited a little while and realised that no answer was coming, he went on, "You wouldn't be trying to help me if you thought I was a murderer, would you? Or would you? Could it be you're grateful to whoever it was who killed your husband for you?"

He saw her head jerk. When she spoke her voice had become suddenly hoarse. "How could that possibly be?"

"Suppose Eleanor comes into it."

"Leave her out of it!"

"I'm not sure that I can. Your husband was doing her harm, deep, psychological harm. He was trying to wreck her life for her, and you could only look on."

"He wasn't succeeding. He'd lost his influence over her. She was going away with Tim."

"Then why do you get so scared if I mention her?"

"I don't."

"You do, Rachel. And it wasn't until after your husband's death that she told you she'd decided to go away with Tim. And perhaps you don't believe she ever did decide it. She doesn't seem so sure now about wanting to marry him."

"I told you yesterday, that was shock. She's got over it already. They're going to get married as soon as they can."

"But I could still be the person who's made it possible and to whom you're really very indebted."

She repeated her soft little moan. "One could almost suppose you want me to think you're guilty."

"No, I don't want that."

"What do you want, then? Are you clearing the ground to be able to prove that Tim or Eleanor's guilty? Or"—her voice grated again—"or that I am?"

She came a step closer to him, tilting her head to peer up into his face. It occurred to him only then that his must be as much of an enigma to her as hers was to him. He wondered if Colin, hidden in the bushes, could see either of them at all, or could only hear their voices. The rain, light though it was, gave the darkness substance. It made it something that you could touch, feel brushing against you.

"You're as good a suspect as I am, aren't you?" he said, but he said it softly, as if he were taking her into his confidence. "You'd motive and opportunity. Tell me, Rachel, why did you come out here instead of Ambrose?"

"Well, you know what he's like. He was in a blind rage about the whole thing. I didn't know what he might have done to Cornelia if he'd found her here. Tim and I talked him into letting me come instead."

"Tim?" Matthew said. "I saw him this morning. I didn't think he knew about the call."

"Of course he knew about it. He was there when it came through. And he told me about having seen you this morning. He couldn't make out if you knew anything about the call or not, but in case you did, he didn't want you to know we'd guessed it was Cornelia's doing, because you'd have told her about it and then she wouldn't have come and we'd never have been absolutely sure we were right. Tim's not such a simple soul as he seems. He's really quite deep."

"Deep enough to disguise his voice and make anonymous calls himself?" Matthew asked.

She raised her hands, locking them together as if that would stop her doing something violent with them.

"*Now* what are you talking about?" she demanded.

"Well, you know Welsh isn't the only person who's had an anonymous telephone call," he said. "I had three and Colin and Cornelia have had two. I thought mine were made by a man, Cornelia thought the one she answered was made by a woman. So mightn't it have been a man and a woman, acting together, who made them, and mightn't they just possibly have been Tim and Eleanor? I've never understood the purpose of those calls. They've never made any sense to me. But those two are practically children, even if they're going to be married soon, and sheer childishness, sheer childish trouble-making without any understanding of the consequences, might be the best explanation."

"Stop it!" Her voice had dropped to a furious whisper, but it interrupted him as effectively as if she had shouted at him. "Have you no sense of reality? You'll be saying next that Ambrose and I got together to make those calls. Go on, say it, why don't you?"

"I hadn't thought of it, but did you?" Matthew asked.

"He and I aren't children!"

"No, and I can't think why you should have done it at all, unless, to go back to the beginning, you honestly believe

I'm a murderer and want me to suffer for it. But that doesn't fit with the way you've tried to help me and doesn't seem like you."

"If you're a murderer, you murdered the wrong man, didn't you?" she said. "Grant didn't kill your wife. You'd no reason on earth to harm him. And if you did it, I wonder how it feels. What a pity you didn't ambush and kill your milkman, then you'd be feeling fine. Oh, I'm sorry for you— not grateful to you, as you think, but very, very sorry for you! Now go away and don't come back or ever let me see you again."

She turned and shot away into the Welshes' garden, slamming the gate behind her.

Colin did not step out from the bushes immediately. He waited until the sound of the door into the Welshes' house opening and closing had reached him and Matthew. Then he thrust his way out on to the path and stood beside Matthew, his hands in his pockets, his chin sunk in the collar of his anorak. He gazed out to sea. There was something abstracted about him, as if he was hardly aware of Matthew's presence, had not paid much attention to what he had been hearing and had thoughts of his own to pursue.

"Well, we might as well be getting home," he said after a moment.

Matthew started down the hill.

"Anyway, Cornelia seems to have been wrong about Welsh," he said. "Or at least, Rachel thinks she was. She's got me tagged as the murderer."

There was no answer from Colin.

Matthew went on, "It's odd, she used the same phrase as Mellish, that I'd murdered the wrong man. I didn't, of course, but it seems to mean something. . . ."

He slipped on the muddy path as he spoke and nearly fell. Colin reached out quickly to help him to his feet, then kept a hand on Matthew's arm, as if to prevent his falling again. Matthew started onwards to the cottage, but found that Colin's hand was holding him back.

"But of course!" Matthew exclaimed. "I didn't kill the wrong man, but the wrong man was killed!"

And suddenly fear flooded his mind, fear such as he had never known before. In the moment of falling he had seen something clearly and at last understood his danger in the darkness on the lonely path. He tried to wrench his arm out of Colin's grasp. It was useless. His strong fingers held on. His hard, muscular body, so much more powerful, so much better trained than Matthew's, thrust violently against it, forcing him towards the edge of the cliff. One arm went round Matthew's neck, jerking his head back so that he was helpless.

"But why—?" he managed to gasp. "Why me—why you—?"

Then there was nothing under his feet and he was falling. The last thing of which he was aware was a strange sense of light and a roaring sound, as if thunder had exploded in the night, then there was only blackness and nothingness.

CHAPTER TEN

A kind, very Irish voice was saying, "It's all right, darlin', it's all over, you're quite all right."

Someone was patting his hand.

Matthew's eyes blinked open and saw a smiling face under a white cap bent over his. He moved his head a little, and realised that it was on a pillow and that even that slight movement hurt a good deal. He was in some place where he had never been before. It was a small, high room with a basin in one corner, some built-in cupboards, one easy chair and a locker beside the bed. He was in hospital, then, and apparently in a private ward. A wave of panic hit him. Could he afford it? Then he remembered that of course he could and he let his eyes close.

But immediately panic surged through him again. There was something the matter with his leg. He could not move it. Did that mean he had lost it?

But the trouble with it was that it felt as if he had too much leg, not too little. The wild fear of mutilation passed as he realised that it was in plaster.

The sister patted his hand again and said, "Just a few bones broken, darlin', nothing to worry about. Aren't you the lucky one?"

He started to ask her what had been broken, but it seemed too much effort to complete the sentence.

As if she understood him, she said, "It's just your ankle

and a couple of ribs and a few bruises and scratches. You'll
be on your feet again in no time at all."

"But how did it . . . ?" he started off again vaguely,
with the same feeling that the answer did not matter.

"How did it happen, darlin'?" she said. "That's not for
me to say. You'll know much more about it than I do. Now
I'd go back to sleep. Have a nice rest and later you can have
a talk to the Inspector. But we aren't letting anyone bother
you just yet, so don't worry yourself about a thing."

Her voice was lulling. So were the after-effects of the anaesthetic that he supposed he had been given. He doubted if
he could have kept awake even if he had wanted to. But,
drifting off to sleep, he had a nightmare. It was one that he
had had at various times throughout his life, ever since the
occasion when Cornelia had pushed him down the stairs.
He had been only six at the time and but for the suppleness
of his young limbs he might have been seriously injured.
Afterwards Cornelia had sat beside his bed and cried and
cried and begged to be forgiven, and he had forgiven her
without fuss because at that age it had seemed an easy thing
to do and, besides, both of his parents had wanted it. They
had been very pleased with him when he had let her kiss
him. But in the night the memory of her face as it had been
just before she pushed him had come back to him and he
had woken screaming. And still that face, if he glimpsed it
in sleep, had the power to terrify him. It had long ago
ceased to be Cornelia's face and had become simply a mask
of evil, but now in the dream that he had in the quiet hospital ward it was hers again, only it was also Colin's and it
was also a skull, shrouded in the hood of an anorak, and the
worst thing about that composite face was its familiarity. It
was a face that he had known all his life. He woke shivering
and sweating.

It seemed to him that he had been asleep only for a few

minutes, but the daylight that he had seen outside the window when he had woken before had faded to dusk and a young nurse was just drawing the curtains. In a corner of the room, on the one easy chair, sat Inspector Drayton.

He looked, as he usually did, as if he hoped not to be noticed. He appeared to have been watching Matthew steadily until he opened his eyes, but as soon as Matthew's eyes met his, Drayton seemed to become interested only in the nurse. Yet Matthew had the impression that the Inspector could see further to the side than anyone he had ever met and that he was being observed as carefully as ever.

The nurse took Matthew's temperature, felt his pulse, made sure that he knew where the bell was, then left them together. Drayton stroked his chin.

"Been having a bad dream?" he asked, sounding as if he had come only to commiserate.

"Yes," Matthew said, "one of my very bad ones."

"Too bad. But I know how it is. I've one or two like that myself. I've had them all my life. One is that I'm in some foreign place and I've lost my passport and all my money. I can't think why I should dream about a thing like that. Maybe the psycho boys could tell me. Actually I've hardly ever been abroad and never lost my passport or my money. But it always terrifies me."

Drayton in this confiding mood was strangely alarming to Matthew.

"Where am I?" he interrupted him.

"In Fernley Cottage Hospital. We put you into a private room because the doctor seemed to think our coming and going wouldn't do the other patients any good. Not that we're going to trouble you too much at present. How are you feeling? Much pain?"

"Nothing to speak of. I think I'm pretty doped. The

room keeps moving around. I don't know that I'll be able to tell you much. Everything's pretty hazy."

"Never mind, it'll come back later. I don't suppose you can remember much of what happened on the cliff."

"Some of it. I remember talking to Mrs. Staveley and then talking to my brother-in-law and then . . ." Matthew stopped. He was confused not only by a partial black-out of memory, but also by a feeling that he did not know how much he wanted to tell this policeman about matters which, after all, were in the family.

He need not have hesitated. Drayton seemed to know it all.

"Then you went over the cliff," he said. "You know, you were dead lucky. If you'd been a little higher up the cliff, nearer the Staveleys' place, where the cliffs are sheer, you'd have gone straight down on to the rocks at the bottom and you'd have been done for, just as Mr. Staveley was. But further down there's more of a slope, so you bounced a bit, and there are some hawthorn bushes sprouting out of a crevice and you landed bang in the middle of them. Not a pleasant experience for you, but all the same, not fatal."

"But how do you know all this?" Matthew asked.

"Well, that's where you were in luck again," Drayton answered. "Young Welsh saw it all."

"But how? Where was he?"

"He was in the garden, just on the other side of the wall, all the time you were talking to Mrs. Staveley. You don't suppose she'd have gone down there all alone to talk to someone who'd been threatening Mr. Welsh on the telephone. Young Welsh went down there some time ahead of her and hid behind the wall and heard you and Naylor arrive. He knew Naylor was there all the time, though she didn't till later. And when she'd gone back into the house, Welsh waited for the two of you to leave, then he heard you shouting and he rushed out. He'd a torch with him and saw everything."

"I don't remember shouting," Matthew said.

"And I dare say you never will. That's the kind of thing you can black out on for good."

"I do remember light, though." Matthew frowned, trying to recall what he had understood so clearly in the moment before his fall.

"In case you're wondering what happened next," Drayton went on, "Welsh tackled Naylor and knocked him out. Naylor's pretty tough for his age, but Welsh is bigger and younger and heavier. Then he called for us, and while some of us were rescuing you from the bushes, I was busy charging your sister and brother-in-law with murder. And that's where you can help us, if you want to."

Matthew's mind was still very vague. "Suppose I don't want to?"

"Because she's your sister? Wouldn't that be carrying family feeling a bit far? She conspired with her husband to kill your wife, then Staveley in mistake for you, and then they had another go at you, and it's just chance that they didn't succeed. They're a very dangerous pair, you've got to admit it, and they'll be better under lock and key. Not that Welsh's evidence isn't enough to convict Naylor for the attempt on you."

"You're sure they killed my wife?"

"Of course. It was her money they were after, wasn't it?"

Matthew tried to lift his head a little, but found that this hurt him in several places at once. Remaining still, he only moved his eyes, looking up at the ceiling.

"That's right. That's what I suddenly understood just before Colin attacked me. That the plot began with his arranging to give me that alibi the day my wife died. He rang up beforehand and asked me to meet him for lunch. He

probably knew I'd be at Welford, among other people, for
the rest of the day, but I might go off somewhere on my
own for lunch, as I often did, and not be able to prove my
innocence. And it was important that I should be able to,
because to suit their plan I had to inherit Kate's money,
which I couldn't have done if I'd been involved in her
murder. You can't profit by any crime you commit, can
you?" He closed his eyes for a moment. "D'you know, it
was just after he'd strangled Kate that Colin came to meet
me and I noticed he was in an odd, nervous state, but I
thought it was because he was going to give a paper to the
Royal Society! Well, the next step was that I had to commit
suicide. I was to come and stay with them here, but be so
depressed that I threw myself off Suicides' Cliff. Such a convenient thing to have in your neighbourhood, a place where
suicides are almost expected. And Cornelia would have inherited the money I'd inherited from Kate. That's the rough
outline of what was planned, only of course it didn't work
out like that."

"Would she have inherited your wife's money?" Drayton
asked.

"Oh yes. Kate and I both made wills when we were first
married leaving everything we had to one another, but we
both put in a clause that if we died at the same time—in an
aeroplane crash, for instance—or without the survivor's having made another will, everything there was to go to
Cornelia. Kate hadn't any relatives she cared about and
Cornelia was the only one I'd got left. Of course, when we
made those wills neither of us had any money to speak of.
Kate only came into her aunt's money last year and I dare
say she'd have changed her will sometime, because I think
in those last few weeks of her life she'd been trying to make
up her mind to leave me."

"She came on a visit to the Naylors in December, didn't

she?" Drayton said. "D'you think she'd have discussed that matter with your sister?"

"She might have. I don't know. But I know Cornelia realised she'd fallen in love with Staveley and probably saw how restless and unhappy she was."

"If that's so, it would have helped them to make up their minds to go ahead with the murder, because it wouldn't have been much good leaving it until after she'd left you."

"No."

"But it puzzles me how Naylor could have mistaken Staveley for you. There wasn't the slightest resemblance between you."

"We were about the same height," Matthew said, "and that evening we were both wearing anoraks, and a quilted anorak is a pretty concealing garment. Staveley was much solider than I am, but it wouldn't have shown inside an anorak. And it was raining, so we both had our hoods up, though his must have blown back as he fell, because his head was bare when they found him on the rocks. The anoraks were different colours, but that wouldn't have shown in the dark. And Staveley carried a walking-stick, as I often did, so when Colin saw him, probably standing still, leaning on the stick and looking out to sea, he could easily have taken him for me. He was expecting to see me there, after all. He couldn't know that I'd walked further than usual and would be coming back along the path some time later than he was prepared for, or that Staveley had had a row with his wife, was rather drunk and was probably wandering about, doing nothing in particular. I imagine too that Colin acted pretty quickly and didn't give himself time to realise his mistake."

"That stick," Drayton said, "you think Naylor grabbed it as he pushed Staveley off the cliff and put it carefully on the bench, as if he'd left it there on purpose, all to help persuade us that your death was suicide."

Matthew gave a faint smile. "Only it had the opposite effect, didn't it? Because the sticks had got mixed up, as well as the victims, you were sure I'd met Staveley that evening and sat on the bench, talking to him, and then killed him. And your suspicion of me was the last thing that suited the Naylors, because if I'd been put away for murder, I suppose Kate's money would have been frozen and they'd never have got their hands on it. So they started a fake hunt for the murderer, trying to point suspicion at Ambrose Welsh and arranging another opportunity to turn me into a suicide."

"Had Naylor realised he'd killed the wrong man before you walked into the cottage?" Drayton asked.

"I doubt it."

"It must have given him quite a turn when you did."

"I think it did. As I remember it, they were both in a rather peculiar state when I went in. My sister looked as if she was ready to start screaming. Then they immediately told me it was because of another anonymous telephone call they'd had. It was a pretty good effort, considering that my footsteps on the garden path could have been the only warning they'd had."

"Ah yes, those anonymous calls. . . ." Drayton seemed about to say something more, then to change his mind. He stood up. "You're getting tired," he said. "We'll leave it for the present. I'll come back tomorrow and see how you're getting on."

"We may as well finish the thing now," Matthew said, though Drayton's words had made him realise how exhausting it was to keep a hold on his thoughts. If he once let go, he felt, there was no telling when he would be able to think lucidly again. "Those calls to me were made by Colin. He disguised his voice very cleverly. The object of them, I believe, was to make me want to get away from that house and come to stay with them, so that they could set up my suicide. The calls Cornelia had were invention. She wanted me to think it must be someone in Fernley making them, to keep me here, trying to find out who it was. She also wanted a reason for blurting out the whole story of them at a party, to impress people with how depressed I was. She also told everyone she met about my depression." A memory suddenly came to him and he gave a dry laugh. "D'you know, there was a time when I even suspected Superintendent Mellish of making those calls to break my nerve. You might tell him that sometime."

"Well, he and I suspected you of murder," Drayton said, "so that makes us even. I'll leave you in peace now. I hope things go all right with you. You're in good hands here. If you think of anything more, you can tell me later."

He went quietly out of the room.

Soon afterwards Matthew was brought a meal consisting of scrambled eggs accompanied by mashed potatoes that had certainly come out of a packet and a pallid jelly. As he had no appetite at all, it did not matter. Later he was brought Ovaltine and given some sleeping-pills and that night he slept peacefully, without dreams.

Next day, after Dr. Parkes had been to see him, Drayton appeared again. With his usual air of apology he took Matthew right through the statement that he had made the day before and asked him if, now that he had had a night's rest, there was anything that he would like to add to it. Matthew had a feeling that there were many things that he had left unsaid, but that none of them was likely to interest the Inspector. He agreed to make the statement again, so that it could be taken down in writing, and to sign it whenever Drayton wished.

His first unofficial visitors were Mr. and Mrs. Richardson, whom Matthew had met briefly at the Naylors' party. Mrs. Richardson was carrying a great bunch of forsythia. Matthew was sitting in his chair by then and was able to hobble about the room.

Mrs. Richardson said, "My husband tells me you don't take flowers to a man, you ought to take books or a bottle of whisky, but isn't that ridiculous? Men like flowers just as much as women do. This is from our own garden. I hope you like it. And I do hope you don't think we're intruding, but we had an idea we want to put to you. I hope it doesn't sound too impertinent and you must of course say no if it doesn't appeal to you."

She had put the forsythia down on Matthew's bed-table and she and her husband had both sat down.

"We were wondering, you see," she went on, "about how you're going to manage when you come out of hospital. Perhaps you've got it all thought out, in which case please take no notice of what I'm going to say, but in case you haven't, we wondered if you'd care for a room in our bungalow till you're able to look after yourself. We've been thinking we'd like to take a lodger to help out with our pensions, and if it would be of any help to you, you could be our first. There's no need for you to answer immediately. We aren't in any hurry. We were going to wait for the tourist season to get properly started, but we could have a room ready for you any time. So just think about it."

Matthew began, "It's extraordinarily kind of you—"

"Not at all, not at all," she said. "A purely commercial arrangement. So don't hesitate to come to us if it would help you. Our granddaughter, the one at Sussex University—d'you remember, we were telling you about her?—is coming to stay with us over Easter, so you'd have some young company."

She went on to chatter about her granddaughter while her husband sat smiling and approving of her, and the two of them presently left without having made a single reference to murder, for which Matthew was so grateful that he made up his mind almost as soon as they had gone to accept their offer and rent their room. Even the thought of having to meet the granddaughter did not put him off. The arrangement would certainly be a great help until he felt able to move into a hotel, and besides that there was the possibility that before he left Fernley he would see Rachel Staveley again.

He had hoped that she would visit him in the hospital, but she did not come, and as the days passed, his disappointment at this grew surprisingly painful. At first he had hardly been aware that he wanted to see her, but gradually it became one of the only things that he could think about.

She came at last on his last day in the hospital. Either she had changed since he had seen her last, or his memory of her had become distorted by the vague dreaming that he had done about her, for she seemed more fragile than he remembered and looked older and more tired. She was wearing the dark red trouser suit in which he had seen her first and a short fur jacket. The skin on her face seemed drawn tight against the delicate bones behind it.

Dropping into a chair, she said, "I don't know whether or not you want to see me after all the things I've said to you, but I thought I'd come to say good-bye."

"But I'm not leaving," he said. "I've taken a room at the Richardsons'."

"Yes, I know, but I'm leaving," she said. "I told you I thought I would. I've managed through a friend to get a job in a bookshop in Newcastle. A nice long way away. I feel I want to get as far away as possible. And I've put the shop here up for sale. I start work on Monday, so I'm leaving on Friday, to give myself time to find somewhere to stay."

"I'd hoped I'd see more of you while I was still here," he said with more dismay than he showed.

"Really?" she said, surprised. "When I almost told you I suspected you of Grant's murder?"

"Only you never really believed it, did you?" he said. "Suspecting me was only a kind of protection against suspecting Tim and Eleanor."

"Perhaps. I'm not sure. Talking to you, it didn't seem possible you'd harm anybody, then I'd start to wonder. . . . And all the time, there was no need for it. But the way it's turned out must be terrible for you—I mean, about Cornelia."

"I'm getting used to the idea," he answered. "I realise, of course, she's hated me all her life. I was very well aware of it when we were children, but she seemed to grow out of it. And perhaps she would have, after a fashion, if Colin had done better in his job than me. Then she could have started patronizing me again and might have borne with me. But she must have known for some time that he was never going to get any further, and so perhaps money came to be the only way of getting even with me. Colin just did as he was told. I don't know how much of it is really my own fault. If I'd understood them both better we could just possibly have come to terms with one another."

"Don't," Rachel said. "You're one of the people who always blames himself for the failures and iniquities of other people. It isn't sensible. It was a cold-blooded crime if ever there was one. Look at the way Cornelia made sure you went up on to the cliffs with Colin. That was the real reason she telephoned Ambrose, wasn't it? After Grant's death you weren't likely to think of that path as a pleasant place for your evening walk, so she fixed an appointment up there for you that you'd have to keep, and Colin's going along with you to see what happened must have seemed quite natural."

"He tried to stop her making that appointment," Matthew said. "They quarrelled when she insisted on going ahead with it. I don't think he wanted a second fall from the cliff."

"If he didn't, it wasn't because he wanted to protect you. Don't start thinking that. You'd have been given an overdose of something, or perhaps died of carbon monoxide poisoning in the garage."

"I suppose you're right. Can you tell me, is it true that Welsh fell in love with Kate when she was here? Cornelia told me he did, but I've no evidence of it, apart from what she said. She wanted me to believe he was so jealous of Kate he killed her and then killed Grant."

"I don't think for a moment Ambrose has ever been in love with anyone but his wife. If she'd lived, what a different person he might be. By the way, he's bought my house. He says he won't risk having another landlord like Grant. He's going to be the landlord now and let it for vast sums to summer visitors."

"What about Tim and Eleanor? What's going to happen to them?"

"They got married yesterday. They've found nowhere to live yet, but they've started looking."

"But you—I'm not going to see you again?"

She twisted her fingers together in her lap, looking down at them.

"Are you sure you want to?"

"Very sure."

"It's a bad sort of time, you know, for trying to build something new. We could so easily clutch at one another for the wrong reasons."

"I know what I want," he said.

"But I'm not sure that I do. I want to go away and—it's such a trite phrase, but I mean it—to find myself. Living with Grant, I haven't been myself for a long time. And I think you should go to Australia and do the same thing. And when you come back, if you still want to, you can find me."

"But how shall I find you? Where will you be by then?"

"Tim and Eleanor will be here. They'll always have my address. But if you find you want to forget everything that's happened here, you needn't come looking for me."

There was a finality in her voice with which he did not attempt to argue, but he held out a hand to her and, taking it, she bent over him quickly, brushing his forehead with her lips, before she left him.